BEHIND CALLOUTS

INSIDE THE MIND OF A BODYBUILDING JUDGE

SUNIL SHEORAN

BlueRose ONE.com
Stories Matter
NewDelhi • London

BLUEROSE PUBLISHERS
India | U.K.

BlueRose ONE
Stories Matter
NewDelhi • London

For permissions requests or inquiries regarding this publication,
please contact:

BLUEROSE PUBLISHERS
www.BlueRoseONE.com
info@bluerosepublishers.com
+91 8882 898 898
+4407342408967

ISBN: 978-93-7018-075-8

Cover Design: Shubham Verma
Typesetting: Sagar

First Edition: June 2025

Author

Sunil Sheoran has spent years navigating the multifaceted world of bodybuilding, both as a judge and coach, bringing a level of expertise and insight that few possess. Sunil's goal is to bring more clarity to the judging process, making it easier for everyone—athletes, fans, and competitors alike—to understand what really goes into those decisions. From the pressure athletes face to the tough calls judges have to make, he wants to shed light on the complexities of bodybuilding. Through his work, he aims to change the way people view bodybuilding, bringing more understanding to the sport and what it truly takes to succeed, both on stage and behind the scenes. He aims to professionalize the conversation around bodybuilding, making the standards clearer, decisions more transparent, and the athlete's journey more deeply understood by those within and outside the sport.

Disclaimer

The information contained in this book is provided for general informational and educational purposes only. It is not intended as, and shall not be construed as, medical, legal, financial, professional, or any other form of advice. Readers are urged to seek independent professional consultation suited to their individual circumstances before making any decisions based on the material herein.

The author and publisher make no representations or warranties of any kind, express or implied, regarding the accuracy, completeness, reliability, suitability, or availability of any content. Any reliance placed on the information is strictly at the reader's own risk. The author and publisher expressly disclaim any and all liability for any loss, injury, damage, or adverse consequences arising directly or indirectly from the use or misuse of this material.

Examples, anecdotes, and personal experiences mentioned are for illustrative purposes only. Any resemblance to actual persons, living or dead, or to real events is purely coincidental. No intention exists to defame, harm, or malign any individual, group, organization, or entity.

All trademarks, service marks, and copyrighted material referenced in this book are the property of their respective owners. All such references are used in accordance with the principles of "fair use" for informational and educational purposes only.

Why This Book?

"**Behind Callout: Inside the Mind of a Bodybuilding Judge**" was born from a need — a deep, undeniable need to tell the untold story from the other side of the stage.

In a world where athletes grind for months, coaches strategize tirelessly, and fans build dreams around physiques, there remains one constant that is so often misunderstood: the judges. We are seen but rarely heard. We are respected but often questioned. We carry the weight of expectation, emotion, politics, and perception every time we raise that scorecard.

This book is my attempt to bridge the gap — the gap between what competitors believe judging is, and what it actually feels like to judge. I wanted to share the reality behind those decisive moments, to walk you through what we see, what we weigh, and what we feel in the pressure cooker of competition.

I wrote this book to open a door that has been closed for far too long — to bring athletes, coaches, and fans into the mind of a judge. To explain not just *what* we look for, but *how* we feel when we look. To explain the standards that define each category, the fine margins that separate greatness from good, and the emotions we carry even after the final callout is done.

I wrote it to offer my perspective, my emotions, my experiences — not as an authority, but as someone who cares deeply about the integrity of the stage.

Beyond the technical side, this book dives into the complaints, the frustrations, and the finger-pointing — not from a defensive place, but from a place of understanding. I unpack the common misconceptions athletes and coaches carry about judging, and offer an honest reflection on the human side of it all.

I also expose the business side of bodybuilding: the glamour, the deals, the federations, and yes, the controversies that we as judges witness first hand. And through it all, I weave in my personal journey — the pride, the guilt, the exhilaration, and sometimes, the heartbreak — that comes with sitting at the judges' table.

I wrote this book because the truth matters.

I wrote it because I believe understanding creates respect.

And I wrote it for every athlete, coach, fan, and aspiring judge who has ever wondered, "*What's really going on behind that callout?*"

If you've ever questioned a decision, doubted a result, or wondered what really happens behind the scenes — this book is for you.
If you've ever loved bodybuilding enough to want to understand it fully — beyond muscle and medals — this book is for you.

Welcome inside the mind of a bodybuilding judge.

Table of Contents

Part I
Stage of Glory

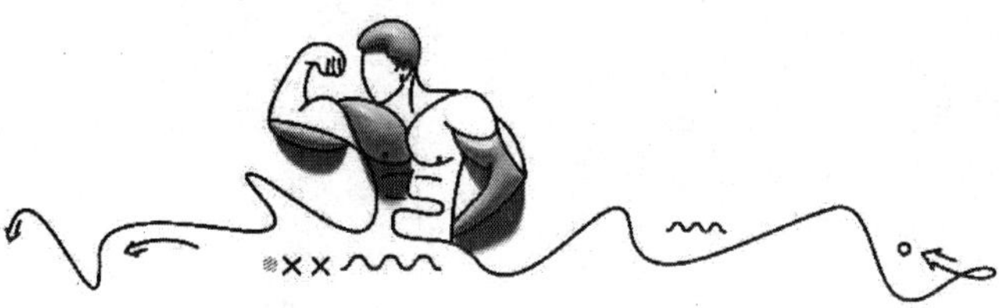

The Unspoken Truth of the Stage

The Pull of the Spotlight

The lights dim. Music thunders through the speakers. A single spotlight cuts through the darkness, and then — silence. All eyes lock onto a figure stepping into the light. Bronze-skinned, razor-sharp, carved like marble. Muscles ripple with each step, veins map across skin like rivers over terrain. Then comes the first pose — and the crowd erupts.

This isn't just bodybuilding.
This is *theatre.*
This is *war paint in oil and tan.*
This is the human body turned into art, refined through hunger, pain, and obsession.

For the audience, it's mesmerizing — a live display of discipline, transformation, and aesthetic perfection. But for the athlete? It's something deeper. That stage is sacred. It's where months of silent suffering finally make noise. Where physical struggle turns into visual glory. It's more than a contest — it's **personal vindication**.

"You're not just stepping on stage to be judged.
You're stepping on stage to be understood — even if no one claps."

— IFBB Pro

There's a reason the bodybuilding stage continues to attract both first-time dreamers and seasoned veterans. It's a place where control meets chaos — where you choose what the world sees. For 60 seconds, you are untouchable, admired, and immortalized in the lens of a thousand smartphones.

And that high? It's addictive.

For the **audience**, the stage is a spectacle. It's theatre. A moment where superhuman physiques are displayed like living statues, flexing with precision, glistening under the lights. Even for people unfamiliar with the sport, there's an instinctual admiration for the discipline it takes to get there. They may not know what "striated glutes" or "quad feathering" are, but they recognize effort. They sense sacrifice.

For the **athlete**, the stage is the finish line — and the reward is visibility. Not just recognition by judges, but acknowledgment of what they endured. Every session of fasted cardio, every gruelling set, every carb-depleted night — all of it culminates in just 60–90 seconds of stage time. And yet, those few seconds are powerful enough to justify months of discomfort.

"Your physique tells a story—of sacrifice, consistency, and unseen effort"

The bodybuilding stage is one of the few places where the athlete has near-total control over what is seen. Lighting is predictable. Poses are rehearsed. Every movement has been practiced thousands of times. In a world that constantly pulls us into chaos, the stage is the one environment the bodybuilder **prepares to dominate** — down to the angle of a toe point or the way a lat spreads.

That control is addictive. Many first-time competitors describe an unexpected rush: the crowd claps, the lights hit just right, and for a brief moment, they become larger than life. That moment becomes the hook — and for many, it's not about trophies. It's about **being remembered**.

What makes the stage even more captivating is the contrast between what people see and what they don't. The audience sees perfection.

They don't see the breakdowns, the missed birthdays, the sleepless nights rehearsing posing in the mirror.

This contrast — between the **effort and the illusion** — is what makes the stage such a powerful draw. It's not just about looking great. It's about making **suffering look beautiful**.

What makes the bodybuilding stage truly captivating isn't just the muscle or the medals — it's the **story behind the body**. The crowd may cheer for a chiseled chest or sharp glutes, but what they're really responding to is the echo of suffering turned into sculpture. The visual manifestation of invisible discipline.

In that moment — under the lights, drenched in applause — the athlete becomes more than just a physique. They become the embodiment of sacrifice, obsession, and unwavering will.

And that's why they keep coming back.
Not just to compete.
But to be seen.
To be remembered.
To prove — if only for a moment — that the pain was worth it.

The Pursuit of Aesthetic Perfection

I've spent years sitting behind the judging table, watching show after show unfold in front of me. I've seen hundreds of athletes walk onto the stage, each carrying their own story, their own struggle, and their own version of perfection. Some came in confident, others shaking with nerves. Some were seasoned veterans with polished routines, and others were stepping into the spotlight for the very first time. But no matter who they were, they all had one thing in common: they were standing under those hot stage lights, hoping to be seen, hoping to be remembered, and hoping to win.

You can see it in their eyes—that flicker of nerves, of focus, of fire—right before the first pose. That deep breath they take, the one that carries every early morning, every missed meal, every ounce of effort they've poured into this moment. And then it happens—they hit that first pose. Lats spread, chest lifted, chin tilted just right. It looks effortless, but we know it's anything but. Because this isn't just about showing up and looking good. This is about trying to look unbeatable. This is about standing up there and saying, without words, 'I belong here.'

And we see you. Every time. We see the hours, the sacrifices, the discipline in how you hold yourself, how you breathe through a pose, how you lock in even when your body wants to quit. It's easy for people to admire the end result, but as judges, we look deeper. We look for the athlete who not only brought the physique—but brought the fight. The one who made the stage theirs. And whether you walk off with a medal or not, that pursuit, that presence, that drive—it never goes unnoticed. That's what this sport is really about. "But here's the catch...

There Is No Perfect.

I've judged athletes with flawless symmetry who got outsized. I've seen freaky mass monsters who got outclassed by a smaller man with tighter lines and better poise. I've watched Bikini girls cry backstage because their "best shape ever" was suddenly "too lean" for the panel.

Why? Because in bodybuilding, **perfection is a ghost** — a constantly shifting, barely-defined ideal shaped by federations, trends, and the opinions of seven strangers sitting with pens in hand.

"He brought size, sure... but the flow was off."
"Her glutes were insane, but the look was soft this year."
"He had the mass, but lacked separations."

We whisper these things during score tallies. Sometimes we argue. Sometimes we agree. But no matter what, the athlete — who sacrificed so much — never hears that conversation. All they see is the placing.

Ask ten judges to define the "perfect physique," and you'll get twelve answers. That's how slippery this concept is.

Symmetry. Proportion. Condition. Flow. Presentation. But even these words fall short. They can be measured — sure — but *felt*? That's where it gets murky. That's where the art begins.

One athlete might be peeled to the bone but lacks balance. Another flows beautifully but fades under bright lights. A third has it all — until they open with a shaky front pose and lose the room's energy.

As a judge, we're trained to score based on criteria. But I'll tell you this honestly — sometimes, **the physique doesn't win. The presence does.** The confidence. The control. The command of the moment.

That's when you realize something haunting:
Perfection isn't found in muscle — it's in mastery.

I've watched competitors walk off stage beaming after taking 5th — because they finally nailed the look they'd been chasing for years. And I've seen champions crumble inside after winning, knowing deep down they could've looked better.

Because you see, this sport isn't just about beating others.
It's about beating *yourself.*
Your old self. Your past physique. Your last prep.
Your own doubts.

Perfection, in this sport, isn't a number. It's a feeling. A fleeting one.

It's not just about victory. It's about making a statement.

Behind the aesthetics is a silent war. Competitors battle food guilt, mirror anxiety, the high of peak week and the crash of post-show blues. The pursuit of perfection doesn't just sculpt the body — it **warps the psyche**. And the scariest part? It's applauded. When someone loses 30 pounds, people say, "Wow, you look amazing." They don't ask what it cost them. They don't ask if they're okay.

From the judge's table, we see that tension. We see the girl backstage with tear-filled eyes, praying she doesn't spill water before going on. We see the guy backstage so depleted he can't finish his rice cakes without shaking. And still… they step on stage with smiles.

It's a sport, yes. But it's also a sacrifice disguised as glamour.

Even when they lose… they return. Again and again.

Because the pursuit becomes addictive. It gives structure. Purpose. Identity. Most competitors will tell you they feel *more themselves* during prep — when life is clean, habits are tight, and progress is visible. Off-season? That's where doubt creeps in.

And so they prep again. Chase harder. Get leaner. Sharper. Closer. They think maybe this time, they'll catch perfection and hold it long enough to earn validation — from judges, from fans, from themselves.

But truthfully? Perfection is never caught.
It's only *approached.*

I've handed out first-place trophies to legends in the making… and I've written down names of nobodies who would later shock the world.

Behind the Posing is a Story

Let me tell you about a Classic Physique competitor I judged not long ago. He had legs like a sculpture, midsection tight as a drum, and posing that could silence a crowd. But what made him unforgettable wasn't just the look — it was the aura.

He stepped on stage and owned it. Not cocky. Not overdone. Just… pure presence. The entire panel felt it.

Later, I found out he had bombed his last show. Didn't even place top 10. But he didn't quit. He went quiet, went dark, went *to work.* The man on stage wasn't just displaying muscle — he was displaying redemption.

And that's when I realized something deeper…

They Don't Want Your Approval — They Want to Be Understood

Most bodybuilders don't chase the stage to be admired. They do it to be *seen* — truly, deeply seen. Not just for their bodies, but for what their bodies represent: discipline, control, resilience.

When they lock in that front double biceps pose, they're not saying, *"Look at my arms."*
They're screaming, *"Look what I've overcome."*

And from the judge's seat, when you *really* pay attention, you can feel it. You can sense the hunger for not just victory, but validation. To know that the 6 a.m. cardio and the weekend sacrifices, the skipped desserts and the quiet breakdowns — were worth something.

Even if just for a nod from the panel.

Even if just for a single clap that feels like a medal.

Identity and the Psychology of Being Seen

From behind the scorecards and beneath the spotlight

You don't just judge physiques.
You judge people's sense of self.

That's the quiet truth no one tells you before you take the judge's seat. When you pick up that score sheet, you're not just ranking bodies. You're ranking **the deepest parts of someone's identity.**

I've watched athletes win trophies and still fall apart backstage because it "wasn't enough." And I've seen others place dead last and walk off smiling — because they finally beat their inner demons just to stand there.

The bodybuilding stage is the most brutal mirror an athlete will ever stand in front of. Under those unforgiving lights, every flaw is exposed. Every weakness, magnified. You can't fake fullness. You can't hide asymmetry. And you *certainly* can't bluff your way through a pose.

But that's just the surface.

The real mirror is internal.

For many competitors, this sport becomes an identity — the only thing they feel they're good at. When everything else in life feels unstable —

finances, relationships, self-worth — prep gives them purpose. And the stage becomes their validation.

I once had a competitor — a Men's Classic guy, beautiful lines, mid-twenties — walk straight up to me after a show and ask, “Was I even worth looking at?”

Not “Did I do well?”
Not “What could I improve?”

He asked if he was worth looking at. That’s how deep this sport cuts.

“Can I get some feedback?”

It sounds polite. But often, it’s not a question. It’s a challenge. Because they don’t want feedback. They want *justification*. They want you to say you were wrong. They want the flaw to be in your eyes — not their physique.

And when you begin to explain — the balance, the posing, the flow, the minor conditioning gap that separated first from third — their eyes glaze over.

They're not listening to *understand.*
They're listening to *argue.*

What you’re witnessing in those moments isn’t disrespect — it’s **cognitive dissonance** in action. A psychological clash between belief and reality.

The athlete **believes** they were at their best.

They **need** to believe they deserved better.

So when the placing doesn't match the expectation, their mind *protects itself* from pain.

It can’t be their fault. It must be:

- The lighting.
- The politics.
- The bias.

- The judges.

Anything but the truth.

Why?
Because the truth threatens the identity they've built around this show. The months of sacrifice. The hunger. The cardio. The sleepless nights.

And just when emotions are most volatile, here come the spectators. The fans. The friends. The supporter holding the gym bag. The coach who thinks he's a guru. The Instagram "expert" who watched the livestream on mute.

They gather around the athlete like armor.

Whispers become gasoline.

"Bro, you were robbed."
"No way he should've beaten you."
"Judges were blind tonight."
"It's all politics, man."

I've seen it so many times. A competitor walks up to us, open to learning — until the corner voices creep in.
And just like that, the rational part of the brain is drowned in **confirmation bias**.

The athlete no longer sees the judge as a guide.
They see us as *enemies to their ego*.

My First Battle for Credibility

I'll never forget this one guy — let's call him Gopi — who had a stunning physique, arguably one of the best in the line-up. But his posing? Sloppy. His transitions? Rushed. His stage presence? Non-existent.

We placed him third — a tough but fair call. He came to me after the show, red-eyed, jaw clenched.

"Tell me why I didn't win," he asked, arms crossed.

I calmly walked him through the notes. Gave him my unbiased opinion. I explained that first and second brought tighter flow, stronger back poses, and more stage charisma.

He just stared. Nodded slowly. Then he said the words that still echo:

"So basically, you just didn't *like* me."

He didn't want truth. He wanted affirmation. And when he didn't get it, he weaponized my objectivity as bias.

That was the moment I realized:
Even the most honest feedback becomes noise when the ego is bleeding.

I wish I could pause time in those moments and tell them:

"I see your effort. I know what it took to get here. I respect your grind. But I have a duty to judge *what is*, not what could have been."

I wish they understood that we aren't their enemies — we're their mirror.
And sometimes, mirrors reflect things we don't want to face.

And just so you know — we *agonize* over placings. We don't casually toss numbers. We debate. We argue. We zoom in on tiny details.

I once spent **ten minutes** with another judge going back and forth over whether an athlete's overall structure was balanced and sharper than the other's — and whether we should weigh the overall balance in Size, symmetry and conditioning.

That's how seriously we take it.

But no matter how precise the process is...
perception is still the villain.
Because to an athlete in pain, no explanation feels enough. No logic feels fair.

Ego vs Self-Respect: The Silent Competitor

The ego shows up long before the athlete hits the stage.

Sometimes, it's subtle — a competitor convinced they'll sweep the division because they won a local show last year. Sometimes, it's loud — the kind that argues with judges, storms off stage, or demands feedback before the results are even announced.

But ego… isn't always arrogance.
Sometimes, it's *fear* in disguise.

I've seen first-timers break down in tears after a show because their entire identity was tied to this one day. They built themselves up for months — maybe years — as *the* future champion. And when it didn't happen, they weren't just crushed. They were *lost.*

They didn't know who they were without the trophy. This is what I tell younger competitors now — and what I wish more coaches preached:

You are not your placing. You are not your prep. You are not your peak week photos or your stage tan or your glute striations.
You are more than the applause you get — or don't get — under those lights.

Because when the sport becomes your entire identity, you're setting yourself up for heartbreak.

I've seen pros walk away because they couldn't mentally survive an off-season. I've seen amateurs grow stronger, smarter, and more confident — without ever winning a show. The difference wasn't their body. It was their *relationship with the sport.*

Why Judging is a Privilege

Let me tell you something from the deepest part of my being — **judging a bodybuilding show is not a job. It's a responsibility. A privilege. A vow.**

It's not about having a good seat, a clipboard, and a mic. It's about holding someone's dream in your hands… and being worthy of that trust.

And that weight?
That doesn't get lighter with time.

When you sit on the judging panel, you're not just watching muscles move. You're witnessing obsession, sacrifice, suffering, artistry, and pride... all packed into a few minutes of posing under cruelly honest lights.

You're watching someone present *the best version of themselves they've ever created.* And they're asking you — to see it, to validate it, to *honor* it.

Who the hell wouldn't feel the gravity of that?

It's a **decision that might shift someone's life trajectory.**

It might be the reason they keep going — or the reason they walk away. It might open a door, secure a sponsorship, earn a pro card, or silence the voices that said they'd never make it.

And if I don't judge fairly, if I let bias creep in, if I favor a friend or a name or a social media following — then I'm not just being unethical...

I'm **betraying the sport.**

That's not a misjudgement. That's a moral failure.

People don't see what we see behind the table. They assume politics. Favors. Manipulation.
And maybe in some corners of the industry, that still exists — and it sickens me.

But not here.
Not where I judge.
Not while I'm breathing.

I judge by **passion.**
By the purity of the sport.
By the *energy* that shakes the floor when someone hits a perfect side chest.
By the *silence* in the crowd when someone flows like art in motion.

If I ever feel myself judging out of habit, or laziness, or bias... that's the day I step down.

Because this sport deserves judges who still *feel something* when the lights go up.

Do you know what haunts me?

Not the arguments. Not the complaints. Not even the backstage meltdowns.

What haunts me are the athletes who walk away quietly — confused, disappointed — but never ask for feedback.

The toughest things I have to say to athletes

''All athletes please go to the green room and better luck next time''

They just leave, thinking maybe they weren't good enough. Maybe the dream isn't for them.

And I wonder:

Did I fail them by not scoring clearly enough? Did I miss something that could've changed their path? Did I do justice to their effort?

Judging isn't just about accuracy.
It's about **accountability** — to the athlete, to the sport, and to your own damn conscience.

Some people think judges only care about first place. That's a lie.

I care about the 7th place guy who brought his best ever package.
I care about the Bikini girl who posed like a pro after battling stage fright.
I care about the Classic Physique competitor who came back this year tighter, fuller, and sharper— even if he still didn't crack the top five.

And— it reminds me *why* I do this.

It's an Honor to Be the Mirror

Being a bodybuilding judge is a sacred role.
You're not the star of the show — but you're the mirror the athlete trusts to reflect their worth.

Not just with kindness.
But with **honest eyes and a steady hand.**

It takes courage to compete.
But it takes character to judge.

And I'll say this loud for every athlete who's ever doubted us:

We don't sit here to break your spirit.
We sit here to honor it.
With clarity. With fairness. With love for the sport.
Even when you hate us for the truth we have to tell.

And So, I Keep Coming Back

Because no matter how thankless it feels sometimes…

No matter how misunderstood we are…

No matter how many times I get blamed, questioned, second-guessed, or disrespected…

I *still* believe in the sanctity of that table.

I *still* believe in this iron-crafted art form.

And I *still* believe — with every rep of my soul —
that **judging is a privilege.**

Conversations I'll Never Forget

They say time heals all wounds, but this sport leaves *impressions,* not just scars.

I've judged hundreds of athletes, at shows big and small. Sometimes… it's not the physiques that stay with me.

It's the *conversations.*

Those raw, vulnerable, explosive, heartbreaking, sometimes infuriating exchanges that happen when the tan fades, and the truth has to be spoken.

Let me tell you about a few that never left me.

"You Don't Know What I Gave Up for This."

It was a regional men's physique show- and honestly, one of the toughest line-ups I have seen in a while. Judging was super tight. Coaches were screaming trunk numbers and the crowd was cheering on every quarter turn.

One athlete, let's call him Sahil, placed fourth. He was good. Really good. But his back shots lacked density and his transitions were stiff. We noted it, scored accordingly.

After the show, he cornered me. Not aggressive, not rude — but you could see it in his eyes: **this wasn't just a competition for him. It was survival.**

He looked me straight in the face and said:

"You don't know what I gave up for this. All my savings are spent on my bodybuilding expenses. I quit my job to prep full time. Without a medal, what would I do now? How can I face my family and start again. I promised my family this time I will get a medal for sure and life will change. And you're telling me fourth?"

I froze.

Not because I doubted the placing. But because I suddenly saw the *life* behind the physique.

He wasn't fighting for a medal. He was fighting to prove to himself — and to the world — that the sacrifices were *worth something*.

I connected with him post show. Gave him honest feedback. Told him how close he was. That day, he didn't cry, but the pain was louder than tears.

That moment taught me:
Every number we write has a story behind it. And we owe it to the athlete to honor that story — even when the outcome hurts.

"Judge Sahab, I Just Wanted to Make My Village Proud."

It was a state-level amateur show in Gurugram. A young Classic Physique athlete came up to me — not asking why he didn't win, not even upset. Just... curious. Nervous. Like a student.

He said, in broken English and trembling Hindi:

"Judge sahab... I just wanted to make my village proud. I'm the only one from there who's ever come this far."

His eyes weren't looking for validation.

He was looking for hope.

I got his message on Instagram and the next day itself walked him through everything. Line by line. Pose by pose. His smile came slowly, like sunrise. Not because I told him he was the best — but because I *respected his effort.*

He sent me a message a year later. Said he started coaching others in his town. Said he still remembers that conversation.

That day, I realized:
Judging is not just about rewarding excellence. It's about nurturing potential.

When ego walked on stage, and logic stayed in the shadows.

This was one of those days.

We were in middle of a Men's Physique division at a regional show — tight category, well-contested, with a clear winner who checked every box: symmetry, stage presence, structure, proportions, and most importantly, **the category-specific criteria.**

But then came the noise. First from the supporters who have nothing to do with bodybuilding and then it came from the **guest of honour** — a well-known senior bodybuilder. A name with weight. A physique that dominates stage.

Sarcastically leaned toward me at the judges' panel and said loudly enough for a few rows to hear:

"Seriously? That's your winner? The crowd is shouting for the other guy. Are you even watching?"

I kept my cool. Years of judging teach you how to smile while someone throws daggers.

Look at him — he's peeled, he's huge, and the audience knows it!"

He turned back and said, *mocking me*:

"Maybe judges need new glasses."

And that's when I had to step in.

I stood up — calm but firm — and walked over. Not to challenge him, but to explain. To **defend the sport** and the integrity of the division. This is *Men's Physique*. Not Bodybuilding, I said. We need to look at the overall structure and a decent waist to shoulder ratio with balanced aesthetics.

He smirked. *"You're just a suit with a pen."*

But I continued, clearly, for everyone to hear:

"This category is not about sheer size. It's about aesthetics. Flow. Conditioning *with proportion and aesthetic.* Most importantly, it's about **presentation**. The athlete you're supporting — does not look aesthetic with optimum ratio, nor his abdomen is clean and tight. He is twisting his torso awkwardly, flexing like a bodybuilder, and not even know how to perform the quarter turns (Men's physique had 4 quarter turns, those days). His back is completely flat without any detailing and muscle density.

I paused and looked at the audience, then back at him.

And in this sport, **rules matter. Categories matter. Presentation matters.**"

That's when it got *ridiculous.*

He looked me dead in the eyes and said:

"I'll go up there myself right now and show you what posing should look like in this division."

I almost laughed. Not out of disrespect — but at the *absurdity. Imagine a 100 KG bodybuilder with waist line of 36 inches confident enough to pose for Men's physique. How tough it is to understand that it's not only about a single variable. All variable go hand in hand and it's the balance that counts.*

Here was a seasoned bodybuilder, decades into his career, acting like he could jump into a completely different division, different posing structure, different judging lens — and win… based purely on **mass and fan applause**.

This Wasn't About the Athlete Anymore. It Was About Ego.

What hurt the most wasn't the shouting or the challenge. It was that **he didn't defend the sport. He used it to fuel his pride.**

He could've supported me as a fellow guardian of the craft — helped educate the audience, explained the criteria, and honoured the athlete's effort while respecting the outcome.

But instead… he became a cheerleader for confusion.

I stood there, letting his words settle. Then quietly said:

"With all your years in this sport, you of all people should be teaching the younger generation about *respecting the division*. Not ridiculing it."

He didn't reply. Just waved me off and returned to his seat

Final Thoughts?

You don't judge to please a crowd.
You don't bend the rules because someone with clout shouts louder.
And you **don't let ego hijack education.**

Judging is a privilege — not just because of what we decide, but because of how we **stand firm in the face of noise, and still serve the sport.**

That day taught me this:
The louder the ego, the deeper the insecurity.
But the louder the truth, the more it echoes... even in silence.

These conversations changed me.

They made me a better judge — not because I adjusted my criteria, but because I deepened my compassion.

I don't have to please anyone—no athlete, coach, or organizer. I'm not here merely to survive; I'm here to serve the sport and help it grow. When you have nothing to lose, you face every challenge with clarity and confidence. Its education and character that give you the right—and the responsibility—to take a stand.

Behind every tan and trophy is a human being — raw, vulnerable, and driven by a dream that often no one else understands. And when they approach you, win or lose, and ask for a moment of your honesty — it's not a burden.

It's an honor.

Because in that moment, they're not just looking for a placing. They're looking for *meaning.*

And as long as I sit behind that judging table, I promise one thing:

I'll always be willing to give them that.

It's about standing tall when people throw shade at your integrity.

It's about holding the mirror to athletes — even when they hate what they see.

It's about making *unpopular* but *right* decisions, and being willing to be the villain — if it means preserving the soul of the sport.

Every time I sat on that chair.
It rebuilt me.

Because if you're going to judge others, you'd better be ready to judge yourself first.

The Champion's Burden

Victory is not freedom. It's a cage wrapped in gold. And the moment you win, you become the one thing you feared most: **a target**.

The audience, they don't know this. They see the spotlight, the perfect physique, the victory pose, and they cheer. But behind the curtains, you feel it. You feel the walls closing in. You are now the standard. The bar. And every day, every single day, you have to remind yourself that you're worthy of holding it.

You thought winning would make it easier. But it doesn't. It just makes the pressure heavier. You're supposed to be untouchable now, right? Everyone expects you to be invincible. You've got the crown, the trophy, the accolades, but in the dead of night, when the world is silent, your mind is anything but.

You know what happens next. You're expected to defend that position. You're expected to win again. And again. And again.

But here's the thing they never told you: the moment you reach the top, the real battle begins.

That's the loneliness of winning. Because when you're at the top, no one sees the cracks. They see the shine. They see the perfect image you present. But behind that image is a person fighting the darkest version of themselves.

But you keep going. Because you have to. Because the **world** expects you to. And that expectation? It weighs heavier than any dumbbell. You'll hear people say: "*You've made it. You're at the top now.*" But you'll also hear, "*Prove it again. Prove it every single time.*"

It doesn't stop. The pressure doesn't stop. The expectations don't stop.

Let me tell you something. **Perfection is a prison**. You can't afford to lose. You can't afford to show weakness. You can't afford to fail. **And in that fear of failure, you lose everything that made you who you are.**

Winning feels great, sure. It's like all those years of hard work, sacrifice, sweat, and pain finally being acknowledged. But then, the world forgets that what you did was once impossible—until you did it. You broke a barrier, shattered a record, and now... it's the new standard. And that's where the trouble begins.

Psychologically, this is a deep and often unspoken battle. Studies in performance psychology show that athletes experience what's known as "**post-victory stress**"—a period where the thrill of winning turns into an overwhelming burden of having to repeat it. The fear of losing your title or position, the constant pressure to surpass yourself, can lead to something much more insidious: *self-doubt*.

If there's one psychological theory that could transform the way you approach your championship title, it's Carol Dweck's Growth Mindset. Dweck's theory is built around the idea that intelligence, talent, and abilities are not fixed—they can be developed through hard work, learning, and perseverance.

Now, let's relate this to bodybuilding. Most people think that once you win, you've made it. But the reality is far from that. The true champion understands that each victory is just another step in their journey. They don't see their success as the end. They see it as the beginning of an even greater challenge.

Branch Warren is known for his no-excuses approach to bodybuilding. He's been through several injuries, including a torn quadriceps and back surgeries, but his resilience in overcoming these challenges is something to admire. After his major knee injury, many doubted his ability to come back to the highest level of competition. But Warren didn't back down. He put in the work, recovering with intense focus and determination, and went on to win the Arnold Classic in 2011. His comeback showed the world that mental toughness and persistence could overcome even the most serious physical setbacks.

Champions use each win to expand their potential, to push their limits further, and to explore new dimensions of their abilities. They know that failure isn't the opposite of success—it's a necessary part of success. Without failure, there is no room for improvement.

There's a saying in sports: "*Motivation gets you started; habit keeps you going.*" But what keeps you going when the spotlight fades? What motivates you to push even when the world stops watching?

Consider **Kai Greene**, one of the most intense and introspective bodybuilders the sport has ever seen. Greene's career in the IFBB was full of pressure: constantly being in the shadow of Phil Heath, despite his artistic approach and incredible physique. His battle wasn't just against Heath or any competitor—it was a battle with his own identity and the way others perceived him. He didn't wait for approval from anyone else. Instead, he focused on his own path, cultivating his **autonomy** in the sport. He didn't let the title of Mr. Olympia define him; he defined himself by his artistry, his approach, and his message.

Psychologists talk about a concept called **cognitive reframing**. It's a tool that helps you shift your perspective when things seem overwhelming. Instead of seeing pressure as a threat to your identity, you can see it as an opportunity to evolve. It's like staring at a mountain that looks impossible to climb and instead of seeing it as an obstacle, you see it as the ultimate test of your resilience.

Arnold Schwarzenegger, after winning his first Mr. Olympia title, he didn't just sit back and relax. He kept pushing himself to improve because he believed that each win was just another step in getting better. When he decided to retire from bodybuilding, he took on a whole new challenge: Hollywood. But it wasn't smooth sailing. He faced rejection after rejection. Instead of seeing these setbacks as failures, he saw them as chances to learn and grow. Over time, his determination paid off, and he became more than just a bodybuilding champion—he became a worldwide icon. This shows how the "growth mindset"—the idea that you can always improve and grow—doesn't just apply to sports. It can shape your entire life, no matter what challenges you face.

The true champion knows that **growth doesn't happen in comfort**. Growth happens when you push past the barriers, when you challenge your limits, and when you learn from every mistake. **You don't just take the burden.** You **own it**. You **use it**. You see the pressure as the fuel for your **growth**, not your destruction.

Bodybuilding: Sport, Art, or Illusion?

"What exactly are we judging — muscle, magic, or make-believe?"

From just few feet away from the stage, I don't see just biceps and vacuum poses. I see *battles*. I see hunger—real hunger—not just for trophies, but for identity. For validation. For becoming someone greater than the reflection in the mirror.

But over the years, that seat has become heavier.

Because I've come to realize... we're not just judging a "sport."
We're not just appreciating an "art."
We're not simply watching an "illusion."

People love to debate whether bodybuilding is a "real sport." To them I say—**spend one week living like a serious competitor.**

Wake up at 5 a.m.

Do fasted cardio before the sun even thinks about rising. Measure every gram of food, every ounce of water. Train while your body begs for sleep, and push through pain that doesn't come with whistles or medical time-outs. Then strip down under bright lights and expose yourself — literally and metaphorically — for strangers to judge you in silence.

There's no luck in this game. No wind to carry a ball. No opponent to blame. It's *you versus you* — and often, that's the most ruthless competition of all.

As a judge, I know how much is behind the physique.

I know the suffering that shaped those lines.

I know the tears shed during peak week, the relationships lost to the tunnel vision of prep, the mental wars hidden behind show-day smiles.

This is a sport. But not like others.
It's not about performance — it's about presence.

Some competitors step onto the stage like statues come to life.

The way they move, hit poses, flare their lats, or twist their torso into a perfectly framed side triceps — it's not just muscular. It's *poetic*.

You realize this isn't brute force. It's choreography.
It's visual storytelling.
Every sweep of the quad, every tight waist, every illusion of size — it's curated.

And it's deeply *personal*.

I've seen competitors who couldn't speak a word on a mic, but tell their entire life story with a routine. Their pain, their comeback, their pride — all poured into 60 seconds of movement under music.

I don't just score the body. I score the *intention*.

I look for that spark — that subtle connection between the athlete and their creation.

Because when it's done right, you don't just see the muscles — **you feel the message.**

But let's not romanticize it too much — because bodybuilding also carries a darker truth.

The illusion is real. And it's powerful.

What the audience sees is peak condition — skin-tight, glossy, tanned perfection.

What they don't see is:

- The diuretic-induced dizziness.
- The cramps backstage.
- The smiles masking anxiety
- The months of body dysmorphia that started long before prep — and will linger long after.

Sometimes, I've watched a competitor who looked like a superhero... then walked past them backstage and barely recognized the same person under normal light.

And that's the danger.

The illusion becomes an addiction — not just for the audience, but for the athlete too.

The stage becomes a drug. The mirror becomes a prison.

I've seen people fall in love with a version of themselves that only exists for one weekend a year. And when that version fades — so does their self-worth.

Judging taught me one thing above all else:

So What Are We Really Judging?

Aesthetics? Symmetry? Proportion?

Yes.
But also — Heart. Presence. Courage.

Because behind the tan, the oil, the number tags — I see *people.*

I see the kid who trained through depression just to step on this stage. The woman who beat hurdles and rebuilt her body from scratch. The father who is chasing one final show before his body gives up.

And I see the illusions they carry — both the ones they show… and the ones they believe.

That's why judging isn't easy.
And why it should *never* be careless.

So is bodybuilding a sport?

Yes — in its demands, its process, and its punishment.

Is it art?

Absolutely — in how it's expressed, revealed, and interpreted.

Is it illusion?

Without a doubt — and it must be handled with awareness and responsibility.

The Blurred Line between Athleticism and Artistry

There's a moment, right in the middle of a routine, when everything slows down.

The music fades into the background. The crowd becomes a murmur. And for just a few seconds, you watch a body not just *pose*—but *perform.*

That's the exact moment you realize: this isn't just about muscle.

This… this is *art.*

Suddenly, the athlete locks in a pose so precise, veins tracing every muscle, and glutes etched like an anatomy diagram. The judge inside me refocuses: conditioning, symmetry, structure, posing.

When a Men's Physique competitor walks with quiet command — chin up, eyes confident, his back spread just right — there's more than posing happening. There's *presence.*

When a Bikini athlete smiles with such conviction that the entire panel feels her energy before she even hits her front pose — that's more than alignment. That's *intention.*

As judges, we're trained to score based on a sheet: proportion, symmetry, balance, and conditioning.

But the truth?
We're human. And when someone's artistry *moves* us, even within the strict rules — we take notice.

That's where the psychology plays its part.

Great athletes *understand* the sport.
Exceptional ones *feel* the performance.

There's a difference between walking out to display a physique — and walking out to *tell a story.*

The best competitors know this. They don't just prepare their body. They prepare their *presence.*

And when they step onto that stage — they become more than athletes.

As judges, we walk that tightrope. We weigh the visible — structure, size, condition — against the invisible — confidence, poise, connection.

And it's hard.
Because how do you *measure* the way a physique makes you *feel?*

But this is exactly what makes bodybuilding different from any other sport.

It's not about being the fastest, strongest, or most efficient.

It's about becoming unforgettable.

Creating an Illusion Through Posing, Lighting, and Presentation

"On that stage, it's not always the best body that wins—
it's the best presentation of that body."

If there's one truth I've learned during all these years, it's this:

Bodybuilding is not always about what *is*—it's about what *appears* to be.

That might sound controversial, even disheartening to some. But it's the game. And to those who master the art of *illusion*, the stage becomes their canvas, the lights their spotlight, and every pose a spell.

Let me share something most spectators don't realize:

The lighting can either crown a champion or bury their physique.

Stage lights aren't soft. They don't flatter you like a selfie ring light. They're intense, high from above, and brutally honest. But when used *intelligently*, they create *depth*. Shadows under the abs. Hard lines around the delts. Drama in the thighs.

Competitors who understand this play with the light. They twist ever so slightly to catch the glare on their best angle. They rotate a touch more to hide weaknesses in obliques or lats.

I remember a young Classic Physique athlete who looked average backstage. Good, but not mind-blowing. But the moment he stepped under the lights—he transformed. His posing was so calculated, so attuned to the angles and contrast that every line popped like comic-book ink. The crowd gasped. Even we judges exchanged glances.

"He knows *exactly* what he's doing."

He didn't grow muscle in 30 seconds.
He manipulated the moment.
That's the *illusion*.

The Power of Posing

A well-executed pose is not a flex—it's *a message*.

You're not just showing a muscle group. You're *selling a masterpiece.*

Some competitors never truly grasp this. They hit poses like checkboxes: "Front double. Side chest. Lat spread." But the best ones? They glide between poses. They understand transitions. They breathe drama into the stances.

I've seen athletes with slightly weaker physiques outrank better-built rivals—simply because they *posed smarter*.

A wide back pose that subtly narrows the waist.

A vacuum that makes the chest look fuller.

A twist in a front relaxed pose that hides a blocky midsection. Or even the *illusion of symmetry* created through angular posing.

I once saw a Men's Physique athlete completely outshine others simply by how he *stood still*.

Yes—*still.*

He didn't fidget. Didn't over flex.

He simply *commanded* presence, chest up, smile sharp, energy electric.

The illusion? He looked bigger, leaner, and more confident than his physique truly offered.

That's *not* luck. That's *stagecraft*.

Presentation: Beyond Muscle, Into Magnetism

You can have the most shredded physique on the planet, but if your walk is weak, your smile forced, or your energy dull—you'll vanish on stage.

Presentation is the final layer of the illusion.

- The tan makes you look harder.

- The oil highlights definition.
- The suit or trunks? Strategic. Color, cut, and fit can make or break balance.
- The walk, the transitions, the eye contact with the judges — *everything* matters.

You know what breaks the illusion instantly?
Insecurity.

I can't tell you how many competitors I've seen who "had it all"—until they stepped on stage and *shrunk*. Their body was there, but *they* weren't.

And on the flip side?

I've judged athletes with average physiques who exuded such charm, confidence, and stage presence that they *stole the show.*
Not because they tricked us.
Because they *believed in their illusion.*

That belief is infectious. And unforgettable. The winners aren't always the biggest. They're the ones who understood the assignment:

"Don't just show your body.
Don't just pose. *Perform.*
Don't just be muscular. Be *memorable.*"

And when they do?

They don't just win a trophy.

They *write their name in the minds of everyone who watched*—including the judges.

And that, is the real illusion.

The Role of Showmanship in Physique Sports

"Muscles get you noticed. Presence makes you unforgettable"

There's an unspoken electricity that charges the air when a great poser walks on stage.

No matter how many shows I've judged, I still get goosebumps when an athlete *owns* the stage — not just with their body, but with their energy, grace, timing, and confidence. This is where *showmanship* transcends sport.

And let me tell you something:
You can't fake this.
You can't teach it in sets and reps.
You *earn* it through understanding the rhythm of the stage, the psychology of the crowd, and the heart of the sport.

In the official judging criteria, you'll find terms like symmetry, proportion, conditioning, posing.

But there's no column that reads "*captivated the room.*"

Yet, as a judge, I can promise you — **we feel it**. When someone steps into the spotlight and everything else fades — *that's showmanship*. And it influences perception more than people realize.

I've seen athletes with near-identical physiques go head-to-head — and the one who *performed* with more presence, fluidity, and style almost always came out on top.

Sometimes, I find myself clapping quietly during an exceptional posing routine. Not because I'm supposed to — but because I *want* to.

There's something magnetic about an athlete who treats the stage like sacred ground. They respect the history. They channel the legends. They make the lights dance off their skin like paint on canvas.

And when you see that...
When you *feel* that...

You don't just judge the routine.
You become a fan.

There are athletes possessing a unique ability to flow like water, turning every pose into an expression of fluidity and grace. These individuals have mastered the art of transitioning smoothly, their movements so effortless that it feels as though their bodies are in perfect harmony with the rhythm of the stage. Every turn, every flex, every shift in position is seamless, as though they're not just performing but telling a story through their physique.

Ed Corney

Watch Ed Corney pose and you're watching poetry in motion. He *danced* with his physique. Every transition was a whisper of art. In the 1977 Mr. Olympia, even while standing next to Arnold Schwarzenegger, Ed *stole the crowd* during his routine. The way he moved was almost hypnotic — smooth, deliberate, theatrical.

Arnold himself once said:

"When Ed Corney starts to pose, everyone shuts up. Even the judges forget to write."

That's what showmanship does.

Mohamed Makkawy

He wasn't the biggest man on the stage, but his lines were beautiful, and his posing was elegant. In the 1983 Olympia, his routine was choreographed to classical music — and for many in the audience, it felt like watching a sculpture come to life. He used light and movement to amplify his aesthetics.

Lee Labrada

Nicknamed "The Mass with Class," Lee Labrada's posing was nothing short of balletic. His routines in the late '80s and early '90s, especially at the 1988 Mr. Olympia, are now used as masterclasses in posing clinics. He choreographed his routines to music that matched his physique — emphasizing control, emotion, and finesse. Labrada's presentation was so tight, so professional, that his routines were often the most replayed moments of the night.

Vince Taylor

Vince Taylor brought theatrics to a new level. His famous "Terminator Routine" at the 1991 Mr. Olympia was unforgettable — mechanical movements, robotic transitions, sudden explosive poses — *pure entertainment with razor-sharp precision.*

Melvin Anthony

Though I never saw Melvin perform live, watching his routines on video was enough to understand the magic he brought to the stage. In the 2003 Mr. Olympia, his routine was like nothing I had ever seen before. His movements were so fluid, almost like he was dancing, but he wasn't just performing; he was showcasing his physique with an elegance that went beyond traditional bodybuilding.

Sergio Oliva Jr.

His posing style stands out because it pays tribute to his legendary father, Sergio Oliva, while carving out his own identity on stage. In the 2020 Mr. Olympia, his routine was a mix of sheer strength and classical aesthetics. Every transition was deliberate, calculated, and smooth, showing his immense size while maintaining incredible control. You could see that he had learned from the best—his father's legacy clearly influenced his stage presence, but Sergio Jr. had taken it further with his own finesse.

Terrence Ruffin – "Ruff Diesel"

Terrence Ruffin pulls you in. He doesn't just hit poses — he performs. Every movement is fluid, every transition thoughtful. You don't see him shift into a pose; you see him flow into it, like a dancer sculpting his own silhouette in motion.

His routines feel like choreography — there's rhythm, emotion, storytelling. He blends Golden Era influences with a modern edge, echoing guys like Zane or Makkawy, but with even more polish. What sets Ruffin apart, truly, is how he transitions. That's where the magic is. There's no stiffness, no reset moments. He glides. And beyond the muscle, it's the expression — he connects.

When Ruff Diesel steps on stage, it's not about size or dominance. It's about art. And that, as a judge, is unforgettable.

Chris Bumstead

He doesn't just show his physique — he presents it with precision and calm confidence. His iconic front double biceps, the vacuum, the flaring lats — it's all deliberate, held with poise that commands silence.

What makes him stand out isn't just the look — it's the timing. He doesn't rush. Each pose breathes. His transitions are minimal, but impactful. He doesn't need theatrics; the elegance is in the stillness. Watching him, you feel the echo of the Golden Era. He doesn't just represent Classic Physique. He defines it.

Win the Crowd, Win the Glory

In a sport that demands perfection, showmanship is what makes it human.

It's the soul behind the symmetry.
The fire behind the front double biceps.
The drama behind the quarter turn.

The greatest physiques may fade from memory, but the greatest performers? They *live forever.*

So if you ever wonder why a certain athlete stood out, why the applause was louder, why the decision leaned a certain way — look past the muscle.

Look at the *showman* behind the muscle.

Because in physique sports, the most powerful weapon is not the size of your arms…

It's the way you make the world *feel* when you flex them.

In a recent show, young Indian athletes—particularly *Delta Dilip* (Men's Physique) and *Sunmeet Gill* (Classic Bodybuilding)—delivered exceptional posing routines that stood out not just for their execution, but for their presence.

Their performances showcased more than physical preparation; they reflected artistry, confidence, and a deep understanding of presentation.

As bodybuilding continues to evolve, so too must the emphasis on posing. It is, after all, the final presentation of an athlete's months or even years of hard work. The ability to connect with the audience and judges through movement, control, and stage presence can elevate an athlete's performance from impressive to unforgettable.

Part II
The Judging Lens

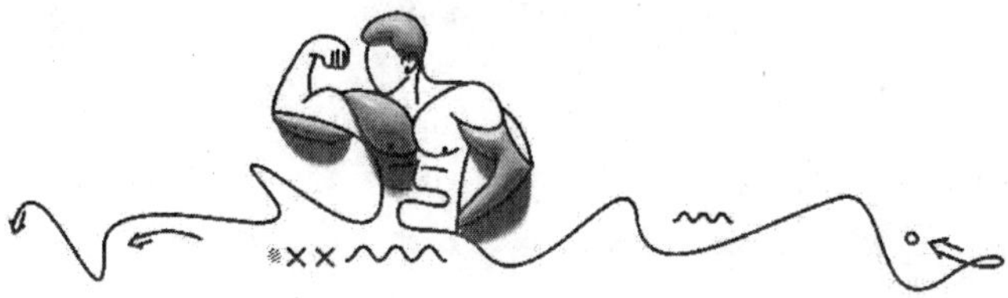

What Judges Actually Look For

You'd think judging a bodybuilding competition is as simple as pointing to the most muscular guy and handing him the trophy. But step behind the judges' table — really sit there, sweat with us under the lights, feel the pressure of a national qualifier or an amateur athlete's dream unfolding in real-time — and you'll quickly understand that **this sport is not one game, it's many games being played on the same stage.**

Each division — whether it's **Men's Physique**, **Classic Physique**, **Open Bodybuilding**, **Bikini**, **Wellness**, or **Figure** — operates under its own language, its own expectations, its own definition of perfection. And if you don't speak that language fluently, you don't deserve your seat.

I've seen athletes walk on stage with phenomenal physiques... and walk off confused, even angry, because they didn't place. Why?

Because they were bringing the wrong weapon to the wrong battlefield.

A shredded Men's Physique athlete trying to flex like a bodybuilder. A Classic Physique competitor who didn't learn how to pose like a classic athlete.

A Bikini competitor who was stage-ready — but not **category**-ready.

Let me give an attempt to **decode** that confusion — to bring clarity where there's so much misconception.

One Body, Many Misunderstandings

One of the most common arguments I hear backstage — and trust me, I've heard them all — is:

"But look at his condition!"
"My athlete had more muscle mass— what else do you want?"

I'll tell you what I want: **the best physique for the division they're standing in.** Not the biggest, not the leanest, not the most hyped. The most accurate. The most appropriate.

You don't bring a sniper to a boxing match. And you don't bring an Open Bodybuilding approach to a Men's Physique competition.

Each division has evolved for a reason. It's a response to what the sport needed — and what the industry could promote.

- **Men's Physique** was born to capture a mainstream, commercial appeal — a look that could walk off stage and into a cover shoot.
- **Classic Physique** emerged when the Open class grew into mass monsters. The world craved symmetry again.
- **Bikini** wasn't just about beauty — it became about flow, femininity, and presentation.
- **Wellness** entered because genetic lower-body dominance needed a home, not just a penalty in other classes.

These divisions are **niches within a niche**, and every athlete needs to understand where they belong — not based on ego, preference, liking but based on fit.

The Judge's Responsibility: Tunnel Vision for Fairness

When I'm seated at the table, I don't care how many followers you have. I don't care what your trainer says backstage. I care whether you **checked every box for your division** — not someone else's.

Each division demands a different kind of eye. As judges, we shift our mindset for every comparison round. We look at symmetry in Men's Physique one way and in Classic a totally different way. The poses change. The flow changes. The narrative of what we're looking for — it changes.

This sport would be a beautiful one if every athlete, every coach, every supporter took some time and pain to truly understand — not assume, not speculate — but understand what the official rule book says, and more importantly, what the judges are actually looking for.

Not what the gym bros think we want.
Not what a viral Instagram reel suggested.
But what the criteria *actually* demand — symmetry, balance, conditioning, stage presence, and division-specific expectations.

If only they paused the noise for a moment and stepped into our shoes — they'd realize we're not killing dreams; we're defending the standards.

We're not blind. We're not biased.

We're trained to protect the **integrity** of this sport. But too often, athletes don't come to be judged — they come to be validated. And when reality doesn't match their expectations, we're the villains. Truth is, this sport could be a masterpiece of discipline, art, and science… if only everyone approached it with **clarity**, not just passion."

Men's Physique

There's something uniquely challenging — and elegant — about judging the Men's Physique category. It's where bodybuilding meets modern fitness culture. It's where structure, poise, and overall image come together to create not just a competitor, but a **symbol of aspirational aesthetics**.

This category is often misunderstood. Many athletes (and even some coaches) still believe that "the bigger, the better" applies here. It doesn't. In Men's Physique, judges are not rewarding maximum muscle mass or extreme conditioning — they're rewarding **shape, symmetry, flow, and presentation**.

Let me try to break it down for clarity.

Symmetry and Proportion

In technical terms, symmetry refers to **bilateral equality** — the left and right side of the physique must mirror each other in muscle development, density, and visual flow.

Proportion, meanwhile, refers to **the relationship between muscle groups**. The deltoids should be round and full. The chest must complement the shoulders, and the midsection should remain tight and clean without being underdeveloped. A well-proportioned physique allows the eyes to travel smoothly across the body, without any single area catching attention for the wrong reasons.

If your quads are bulging under your board shorts and your upper body lacks width — you may be muscular, but not proportionate. If your arms overshadow your chest or your waist breaks the V-line — it disrupts the harmony.

The Aesthetic V-Taper

A **classic V-taper** is the golden standard of Men's Physique. It's a visual shape — not just muscle — created by:

- Wide clavicle structure enhanced by developed deltoids and lats
- A high, narrow waistline free from bloat or thickness
- Controlled obliques that accentuate the taper without "blockiness"

This V-taper should be visible from both the front and back mandatory poses. Judges aren't just evaluating muscles — they're evaluating how your body holds structure under light and posture. A flat back or overextended ribcage can break the illusion. This is where **postural control and posing mechanics** come into play.

Muscle Development

Muscle development in this division is often misunderstood. The criteria demand **clean, athletic musculature with visual fullness** — not density, graininess, or excessive striations.

Judges look for:

- Rounded deltoid caps with defined shoulder tie-ins
- Upper chest development that creates height and depth
- Arms that flow with the physique, not overpower it
- Abdominals that are clearly visible, but not deeply carved or dehydrated

Over-muscular physiques with heavy vascularity, or dry, papery skin — all suggest a level of conditioning that goes beyond the class requirement.

Conditioning

Conditioning in Men's Physique is about being **lean but healthy** — enough definition to reveal muscle separation and abdominal structure, but not so dry that the body looks depleted.

We look for:

- Visible six-pack abs and tight obliques
- Clear muscle separations in the arms and shoulders
- No extreme vascularity, sunken eyes, or deep striations

From a technical standpoint, ideal conditioning sits around **5–7% body fat**, but the visual presentation matters more than the number. A tight, photo-shoot ready look is perfect. Anything more extreme begins to resemble Classic or Open divisions — and may lead to mark-downs.

Posing and Presentation

This division only requires two mandatory poses — **front and back**. These two poses must be executed with **complete mastery**.

In the **front pose**, we look for:

- Shoulder width and chest openness
- Controlled abdominal engagement (without over-flexing)
- Arm spacing that creates aesthetic flare
- Chin positioning, smile, and head control

In the **back pose**, we assess:

- Lat width and activation
- Shoulder posture and waist control
- How well shorts fit (yes, even that matters!)
- Glute-ham tie-in visibility under the fabric (not over-defined)

Transitions should be smooth — judges take mental notes on posture, movement control, and how an athlete manages stage space. Over-posing, unnecessary movements, or exaggerated classic-style routines don't belong here. *Elegance wins over aggression.*

Overall Presentation

In Men's Physique, everything that seems "minor" is *actually major.*

- **Shorts** must be regulation length (above the knee), fitted well, and not distracting
- **Tan** must be even, smooth, and natural to enhance the presentation
- **Grooming** includes hair, nails, skin prep, even facial expressions

From the moment you walk on stage to the final callout, you're being watched. Judges are humans — they respond to presence, confidence, and control. Slouched posture, awkward smiles, or overly intense expressions can damage the visual impact of an otherwise excellent physique.

Judging Framework Summary – Men's Physique Division

Evaluation Area	What Judges Are Looking For
Symmetry & Proportion	Balanced left/right development, muscle harmony, smooth visual flow across all regions.
Aesthetic Structure	Strong V-taper, visual shape that pops in front and back poses, tight and clean waist.
Muscle Development	Full, round muscles with proper volume; aesthetic density without hardness or extreme cuts.
Conditioning	Lean and athletic; defined but not overly shredded; skin tone must appear healthy and polished.
Posing & Presentation	Executed front and back poses with control, charisma, and stage composure; no excessive motion or flexing.
Stage Appearance	Well-fitted board shorts, professional grooming, smooth tan, confident walk, clean transitions, and total polish.

This is what truly defines the Men's Physique class. It's a celebration of balance, class, and controlled power. And when an athlete gets it right — when everything clicks under the lights — the effect is breath-taking.

Classic Physique

It is the division that pays homage to the golden era of bodybuilding — to Zane, to Reeves, to the Greek statues that defined symmetry long before dumbbells existed.

When I judge Classic Physique, it's not just about muscle — it's about balance, structure, and flow. This division isn't just built in the gym — it's sculpted in motion, polished in posing, and brought to life through presence. And yes, there's a *technical science* to it all. Let me walk you through it.

Structure and Height-to-Weight Ratio

As of 2025, the IFBB Pro League has established specific height and weight limits for the Classic Physique division. These limits are designed to promote a balanced and aesthetic physique, encouraging athletes to maintain proportions reminiscent of the sport's golden era.

IFBB Pro League Classic Physique Height & Weight Limits (2025)

Height (up to and including)	Max Weight (lbs)	Max Weight (kg)
5' 4" (162.6 cm)	167 lbs	75.7 kg
5' 5" (165.1 cm)	172 lbs	78.0 kg
5' 6" (167.6 cm)	177 lbs	80.3 kg
5' 7" (170.2 cm)	182 lbs	82.6 kg
5' 8" (172.7 cm)	187 lbs	84.8 kg
5' 9" (175.3 cm)	194 lbs	88.0 kg
5' 10" (177.8 cm)	202 lbs	91.6 kg
5' 11" (180.3 cm)	209 lbs	94.8 kg
6' 0" (182.9 cm)	217 lbs	98.4 kg
6' 1" (185.4 cm)	224 lbs	101.6 kg
6' 2" (188.0 cm)	232 lbs	105.2 kg
6' 3" (190.5 cm)	239 lbs	108.4 kg
6' 4" (193.0 cm)	246 lbs	111.6 kg
6' 5" (195.6 cm)	253 lbs	114.8 kg
6' 6" (198.1 cm)	260 lbs	117.9 kg
6' 7" (200.7 cm)	267 lbs	121.1 kg
Over 6' 7" (200.7+ cm)	274 lbs	124.3 kg

Note: Federation-specific variations may exist, but the principle is universal: balance over bulk.

This technical rule ensures that the athlete must build within artistic boundaries.

Symmetry, Proportion, and Shape: The Golden Triangle

Classic Physique is judged heavily on what we call the **Golden Triangle of Aesthetics**:

- **Symmetry:** Balanced development across both sides of the body.
- **Proportion:** Muscle groups must flow — legs to upper body, arms to shoulders, torso to waist.
- **Shape:** The overall visual silhouette must resemble a V-taper crowned with flaring quads and tight abdominals.

There's a harmony to the look. Judges want to see a physique that flows —You might have big arms, but if your lats don't sweep or your legs don't balance them out — it breaks the illusion. Classic is **all about the illusion** — of perfection, of flow, of golden-era grace.

Muscle Development: Not Just Size — But Lines and Flow

In Classic, muscle is built with intention. It must be:

- **Full but aesthetic** — not overly grainy or dry
- **Separation-focused**, showing clear divisions between muscle bellies
- **Sweeping quads, flaring lats, peaked biceps** — the classic tools of proportion

Your back should pop in a front double biceps. Your legs should tell a story from the front and the side. Your arms should sit neatly within your frame, not hijack it.

A thick waist, blocky abs, or overpowering muscle bellies can all work *against* you here. **Less can often be more**, if it's sculpted correctly.

Conditioning: Crisp, Clean, and Controlled

Conditioning in Classic Physique is where art meets detail. We're not looking for dehydrated, overly striated physiques — that's more in line with Open Bodybuilding.

Instead, judges reward:

- Dry, clean separation in muscle groups
- Visible striations in quads, glutes, delts — but not excessive
- Tight skin, healthy glow, not paper-thin or worn-out texture
- No distension or bloat — control of the midsection is key

From a body fat standpoint, Classic competitors usually hit the 4–6% range. But again, it's not about numbers — it's about how you *look under the lights*. **Are you crisp, composed, and clean? Or overcooked and flat?**

Posing: Where Classic Truly Comes Alive

This is what separates Classic Physique from every other division: **mandatory posing rounds plus the individual posing routine**.

Mandatory Poses (per IFBB Pro League):

- Front Double Biceps
- Side Chest
- Back Double Biceps
- Abdominals and Thigh
- Favorite Classic Pose (unique to this division)

Each pose is judged on:

- Muscle execution and fullness
- Transitions and flow between poses

- Balance and symmetry in each angle
- Facial expression, posture, control

The Routine:

This is where the athlete becomes a performer. You have 60 seconds to create emotion, control, and *connection*. Judges want to see the athlete tell a story — showcasing strengths, hiding weaknesses, and capturing the elegance of bodybuilding's roots.

Some of the best routines I've judged were not the most shredded or most muscular competitors — they were the ones who **connected to the music**, moved with grace, and expressed every pose with intent.

Presentation: The Final Layer of Polish

Presentation includes:

- **Classic trunks**: high-waisted, solid color, fitted properly
- **Tan and skin tone**: smooth, matte finish; no smears or patches
- **Grooming**: clean shave, tidy hair, skin preparation
- **Confidence and presence**: from walk to exit, you must hold the stage

Classic demands **discipline in detail** — everything counts, because the illusion must be perfect from every angle.

Summary – Classic Physique Division

Judging Criteria	What Judges Evaluate
Symmetry & Proportion	Balanced development; visual harmony from head to toe; Golden Era silhouette
Structure	Height-to-weight compliance; taper, torso length, and leg balance
Muscle Quality	Full, separated, aesthetic muscle; not over-matured or bulky
Conditioning	Dry, clean look; visible separations without excessive hardness
Mandatory Posing	Executed with grace, poise, and balance; mastery of transitions
Individual Routine	Storytelling through movement; original, artistic, and expressive posing flow
Presentation & Polish	Proper attire, grooming, stage confidence, and control from entry to exit

Bodybuilding

Bodybuilding is the **undisputed apex** of the sport. This is the division where limitations don't exist. When these athletes walk out, you're not just looking at muscle; you're witnessing **years of discipline, structure, and transformation** come to life on a stage.

This category isn't for those chasing trophies — it's for those chasing legacy.

This division has always been a test of our own observation and respect for the sport. The level of detail, comparison, and fairness expected is unmatched. One misjudged call can impact an athlete who's spent a decade preparing for this very moment.

Muscle Mass – But Not Just Quantity

Yes, **mass matters**, but only when it's mature, dense, and proportionate.

- We look for **complete muscle development**, not just bulk.
- Mass must be distributed **symmetrically** — top to bottom, left to right.
- No body part should overpower another. A huge upper body and underdeveloped legs? That's a no-go.

And yet, it's not about being the biggest man on stage. It's about being the **most complete package**.

Symmetry & Proportion

A well-built body should feel **balanced and seamless**. We assess:

- Left-to-right symmetry: Are both arms, legs, and shoulders equally developed?
- Proportion: Do the quads match the width of the shoulders? Does the waist taper cleanly into the V-taper?
- Flow: Are there aesthetic lines that guide the eye smoothly?

Conditioning

Conditioning separates contenders from champions. It's the **refinement of the physique**.

What we judge:

- **Dryness** of the skin — tight, paper-thin, showing every fiber
- **Striations** — in delts, chest, glutes, and hamstrings
- **Separation** — clear visual distinctions between muscle groups
- **No water retention** — a watery or soft look kills even the best structure

In Open Bodybuilding, if your **glutes and hams** aren't dialed in, it's a sign that you haven't reached the peak.

Stage Presentation

Here's the truth: many athletes lose their placing not because of muscle — but because of **how they show it**.

We're observing:

- **How confidently they hold each mandatory pose**
- Smoothness of transitions — no stumbling, no awkward shuffling
- Control of breathing, expression, and energy on stage
- Ability to **draw the eye** even in a full lineup

Mandatory Poses

Each pose gives us insight into a specific part of the physique. Here's what we're actually evaluating:

Pose	Judging Focus
Front Double Biceps	Taper, arm peaks, quad sweep, abdominal control
Front Lat Spread	Shoulder width, lats flare, chest and waist balance
Side Chest	Chest & upper body thickness, arm size, hamstring tie-ins
Side Triceps	Triceps detail, core tightness, glute-hamstring line
Rear Double Biceps	Back density, traps, symmetry, glutes, hamstrings
Rear Lat Spread	Width and depth of lats, lower back thickness

Pose	Judging Focus
Abs and Thigh	Abdominal detail, quad lines, waist taper
Most Muscular	Overall mass, conditioning, confidence

Every pose tells a story. And believe me — we're reading every page.

It's never about a single muscle group.

Sometimes, the most "massive" guy doesn't win. The athlete with the **cleaner, more aesthetic, and complete physique** — who executes their posing like a professional — will often take the crown.

Every athlete who steps into this division must be prepared to be judged from every angle, under the harshest lights, with **no margin for error**.

Bikini, Figure & Wellness

From the outside, these divisions often get misunderstood. People see sparkle, bikinis, heels, and smiles — and assume it's just a pageant. But from the judge's chair, we see something very different.

We see athletes who've spent months mastering the tiniest transitions, obsessing over symmetry, refining glute fullness, shoulder width, hamstring tightness — all while maintaining femininity, grace, and charisma. It's a fine line: too hard and you're marked down, too soft and you disappear.

I've seen careers made on how an athlete turns their shoulder. I've also seen heartbreak in the eyes of someone who trained like a lioness, but prepped for the wrong division.

Bikini is not about muscle mass — it's about **shape, symmetry, and grace under the spotlight**. This division celebrates the athletic female body without harsh muscle definition. The look must be soft, feminine, and stage-ready — not muscular, dry, or vascular.

But don't let the word "soft" fool you — Bikini is brutally competitive. Placings often come down to **millimeters** and **minor cues** — from posing transitions to the curve of the glutes to how the bikini suit fits on stage under lighting.

- **Overall Shape & Symmetry**: Balanced shoulders, narrow waist, and rounded glutes. No overpowering muscles or overdeveloped traps/delts.
- **Conditioning**: Lean, tight, and toned. No striations, visible veins, or hard muscle separation. Abs may be faintly visible, but not deeply carved.
- **Glutes & Lower Body**: Glutes must be full and lifted with good projection. Hamstrings and outer quads should be toned but not ripped.
- **Upper Body**: Shoulders can be lightly capped but without separation. Arms should look sleek, not striated.
- **Skin, Hair & Makeup**: Skin tone must be even and tanned, suit color should complement physique and complexion. Hair and makeup contribute to overall presentation.
- **Posing & Presentation**: This is where 80% of the battles are won. Judges look at poise, transitions, posture, eye contact, and charisma. Routine must flow with elegance.

Figure represents structured muscularity and shape with an emphasis on symmetry, proportion, and poise. It's more muscular and conditioned than Bikini, but not to the level of Physique. This is where the female body is celebrated as a symmetrical sculpture, not just an aesthetic figure.

- **V-Taper Excellence**: Wide delts, narrow waist, flowing lines from the lats. This is the architectural highlight of Figure.
- **Back Development**: The rear pose is the *money shot*. Rhomboids, traps, teres, lower lats — we need clarity and density, without striations.
- **Legs**: Quads should show shape and mild separation. Hamstrings should be full and defined, but not dry.

- **Glutes**: Full, round, and defined — glute-ham tie-ins visible, but not striated.
- **Conditioning**: Sharper than Bikini, softer than Physique. Muscular separation yes, but **no shredded look**.
- **Presentation**: Figure requires strong static posing — front, back, and quarter turns. No fluid transitions like Bikini. Here, **poise, control, and balance** define professionalism.

Figure is often decided by the back pose. Many athletes build beautiful quads and delts, but falter when they turn around — either their back detail is lacking, or they can't control the pose without shaking or leaning. Stability and symmetry from behind — that's Figure gold.

Wellness celebrates **lower body dominance** — ideal for athletes with naturally more muscular legs and glutes. Think: **strong, curvy, powerful physiques** that reflect balance **from the waist down**, while keeping the upper body elegant and understated.

It caters to women with genetically dominant lower bodies — strong glutes, dense thighs — while maintaining upper body softness and elegance.

- **Lower Body Development**: Glutes are the centerpiece. Full, round, lifted — from every angle. Quads should sweep without looking too dry or hard.
- **Upper Body**: Less developed than Figure. The shoulders can be rounded but should not outshine the lower body.
- **Conditioning**: Lean but not sharp. Some separation is visible in legs and glutes, but no striations. Glutes should look full and athletic, not peeled.
- **Midsection**: Flat and tight. Six-pack abs are discouraged. Obliques and serratus should not overpower the waistline.
- **Presentation & Posing**: Stronger transitions than Bikini. The walk is more assertive, the attitude more athletic. Hands-on-hips, glute-centric back poses, and confident facial expressions dominate.

Comparative Snapshot

Criteria	Bikini	Figure	Wellness
Muscle Mass	Light, toned	Medium, defined	Lower body dominant
Conditioning	Soft, Lean and firm	Lean with separation	Lean legs, full glutes
Glutes Focus	Full and round	Balanced	Central feature
Back Development	Minimal	Highly judged	Moderate
Upper Body	Feminine, no striations	Developed shoulders/back	Capped delts, softer arms
Posing Style	Flowing, graceful	Static, sharp	Confident, assertive
Core Appearance	Flat, subtle abs	Defined core	Flat, tight, not six-pack
Stage Walk	S-curved, elegant	None (quarter turns only)	Powerful, glute-driven walk

To judge these divisions fairly, you must understand that you're not just evaluating physiques — you're evaluating **category alignment**, **execution**, and **presentation mastery**. There's nothing more disheartening than seeing an incredible athlete miss the mark because they prepped like a Figure athlete for a Bikini show. Or because they trained for Wellness but posed like Bikini.

My job is to honor the division, not the individual. And the ones who win are those who **understand that bodybuilding — in all its forms — is a sport of details.**

Fitness Division

The Fitness division is arguably the most demanding of all female bodybuilding categories — not just physically, but mentally, emotionally, and technically. Unlike other divisions where physique is the sole judging criterion, here the score is split between a **physique round** and a **routine round**, making it a true hybrid of aesthetics and athleticism.

This is where **performance meets polish**, and where an athlete must not only build a world-class physique — she must also be a **dancer, gymnast, and show-woman** rolled into one. Its beauty, grace, strength, endurance, and expression — all in a two-minute window.

Physique Round — Aesthetic Excellence

The physique round in Fitness is judged similarly to Figure — though slightly less muscular and with more emphasis on **balance, flow, and femininity**. The athlete must maintain the appearance of a fit, powerful, yet aesthetically appealing physique that complements her athletic abilities.

Judging Criteria:

- **Symmetry and Balance**: Upper and lower body harmony is essential. Shoulders should taper into a narrow waist, flaring out into tight, strong legs.
- **Muscular Development**: Not overly dense — think lean, athletic muscle. Vascularity and striations are discouraged.
- **Conditioning**: Clean lines, visible separation, but not overly dry. The physique should reflect athleticism, not hardness.
- **Presentation**: Quarter turns are performed to assess overall shape, poise, and control. Athletes must present their body with confidence, grace, and polish.

Routine Round — The Performance Factor

This is where Fitness truly separates from the rest of the pack. The routine round accounts for **two-thirds** of the final score at most shows, making it the **primary deciding factor** in placing.

Here, competitors perform a choreographed fitness routine lasting **up to 2 minutes**, incorporating mandatory elements like:

✅ Mandatory Routine Elements:

- **Push-up Variation**
- **High Kick**
- **Straddle Hold**
- **Side Split**

But it's not just about checking boxes — it's about how creatively, cleanly, and confidently those elements are blended into the routine.

Performance Criteria:

- **Athleticism**: Strength, flexibility, agility, and explosiveness.
- **Creativity**: Original transitions, surprising moves, and seamless flow.
- **Execution**: Precision in movement, clean landings, and fluid choreography.
- **Personality & Energy**: Crowd engagement, facial expressions, musicality.

Politics, Subjectivity, and Favouritism in Judging

"Every athlete deserves a fair stage.
Every judge carries the weight of that truth."

"Was that decision fair?"

It's whispered from the crowd, muttered by disappointed athletes backstage, sometimes screamed by overzealous supporters. I've had to live with the weight of those eyes, those questions, and — at times — those accusations. Because the truth is: **this sport is subjective by nature**, and when you combine subjectivity with human emotion, you're always walking a tightrope between clarity and chaos.

Let's not sugar-coat it: **politics exist** in this sport. This isn't a fairy tale.

There are federations with preferred athletes. Coaches with influence. Sponsors who expect returns.

I've seen it. I've felt it.

The Whisper That Shook Me

I was invited to judge a federation affiliated show-- A not so famous federation with people joined together from different states, and they were trying to build their name in the sport. I was asked to be on the panel — probably because they knew my presence would add value, credibility, maybe even attract more athletes. After all, a show becomes "big" not just because of the stage or the lighting — but because of who's judging, what level of athletes are competing, and what kind of cash rewards are on offer.

The event had everything going for it: a good turnout, promising athletes, well-lit stage. Everything felt in place... until that quiet moment backstage. But then... the organiser walked up to me during the show. Calmly. Casually. Smiling.

He held a folded slip in his hand. Nothing unusual.

He leaned slightly toward me and whispered,

"Trunk number X is our athlete. If he's deserving, look into it."

That sentence might seem innocent to many. But if you've ever been in a judge's chair, you know exactly what that sentence means.

It wasn't a request.
It wasn't a suggestion.
It was a polite, subtle way of saying,
"Give him some edge... if he's close, push him ahead."

I was blank for a few seconds, not because I didn't understand — but because I knew exactly what was being said without being said.

This is how **controlled bias** works. Not always loud. Not always forceful. Sometimes it comes wrapped in courtesy.

Let me explain how this plays out in the judge's mind.

When an organiser — the very person hosting the event — makes a suggestion, even subtly, it creates an internal conflict.

This is how **emotional pressure** begins to influence **technical judgment**. And in a sport where subjective scoring already exists — a small push can swing rankings.

This is **not blatant corruption** — it's a **relationship trap**. Judges begin to favor athletes just to stay in the organiser's good books. It's silent. It's unspoken. But it's real.

I took the slip, gently, and placed it under my notepad. Not because I agreed… but because I didn't want a scene. I nodded respectfully, but in my mind, I'd already made a decision:

I'll judge as per the rule book.

Not the whisper. Not the slip. Not the politics.

When Trunk No. X came on stage, I looked at him with a fresh set of eyes. And the truth was — he wasn't ready. His physique lacked balance. His posing was awkward. His midsection was bloated, may be few pounds of fat or spill over due to over loading of carbohydrates.

When the results were declared, his name wasn't in the top three.

And the organiser's smile faded in an instant.

He didn't say anything… but his silence said everything.

I knew right then — I probably wouldn't be invited to their next show. And I was okay with that.

Why am I sharing this with you?

Because this sport won't grow unless we talk about the cracks.

Athletes deserve transparency. They train for months, sacrifice food, money, time, and social life just to stand on stage for 60 seconds. And those 60 seconds should be judged *fairly*, not influenced by who's backing them or what the organiser whispers behind the curtain.

Bias isn't always loud.

It doesn't always come from bad people.

It comes from silent expectations, from relationship pressure, from judges who are afraid to lose their spot.

But what gets lost in the process is **credibility**.

Let's Talk Science for a Moment

As human beings, we are naturally wired to lean toward people who are nice to us — it's called **reciprocity bias**.

When someone does us a favor, gives us an opportunity, or invites us into their circle — we subconsciously feel the need to repay them.

In judging, this becomes a **dangerous lens**. Because you stop seeing with your eyes... and start seeing with your bias.

So What's the Solution?

The only solution is *moral accountability*.

If you're a judge, you need to ask yourself every time:

- Am I scoring what I *see*, or what I've been *told* to see?
- If I had no pressure, would I still give the same rank?
- Can I sleep peacefully knowing I judged honestly?

Because once you compromise for one athlete, one organiser, one federation — you've opened the door to chaos. And you've let down every other athlete who played by the rules.

Every time I sit at that table, I remind myself:

- You're not here to impress the federation.
- You're not here to please the crowd.
- You're not here to serve anyone's agenda.

You're here for the athlete.

For the one who wakes up at 4 a.m., trains through pain, eats from Tupperware, and dares to be vulnerable under stage lights. That's who we owe the truth to.

Federation loyalty and behind-the-scenes influence

Each bodybuilding federation has its unique vision, identity, and approach to athlete development. Some federations are relatively new and strive hard to make a mark. Others have established legacies. In such an environment, standout athletes often become unofficial ambassadors — their presence draws attention, builds reputation, and enhances the overall appeal of the federation.

Is there admiration for such athletes? Certainly.

Does it sometimes feel like their performances are watched a little more closely — perhaps even with higher expectations or more generous interpretations? It can happen. Not out of bias, but because excellence tends to carry influence, and influence tends to shape expectations.

As judges, we're trained to stay focused on the criteria — to assess what's presented, not what's presumed. But we also acknowledge that athletes with strong reputations sometimes walk in with more than just muscle — they carry the weight of expectations, history, and reputation.

It's no secret that many judges in our industry wear multiple hats. Some are coaches, mentors, or even federation officials. That's the nature of a sport that's still growing — passion often takes people down multiple avenues.

But when those roles overlap, it can create tricky optics.

An athlete coached by a judge might feel additional pressure. Other athletes may perceive an advantage, even when none exists. The truth? Most judges I've worked with strive to remain fair and detached during scoring — regardless of affiliations. But fairness alone isn't always enough — *the appearance* of fairness is just as crucial.

Transparency, panel diversity, and structured score tabulations help maintain credibility. It's a shared responsibility — judges, organisers, and federations must work in tandem to keep the sport's reputation strong.

I recall an event where the organiser casually approached during a break. We were mid-show, the athletes giving it their all. With a calm smile, he said, "That one's our athlete —he won few overalls and he will win this as well, focus on his lower body." It wasn't a demand. It wasn't even improper. Just a suggestion wrapped in goodwill.

These things happen. In any sport, local favourites and federation hopefuls exist. But what matters is how we, as judges, respond. I appreciated the organiser's passion — he wanted his athlete, his federation to shine. But I also knew that my role was to evaluate physiques, not affiliations.

And sometimes, the best way to respect someone's trust is by *not giving in to it blindly*.

If there's one thing I've learned, it's that **bodybuilding is more than a sport of symmetry — it's a sport of trust**. The audience trusts us to be fair. Athletes trust that their effort will be honoured. And we, as judges, carry that trust quietly with every score we give.

Is there influence in this sport? Yes — just like in any judged sport. But with the right values, transparent systems, and mutual respect, we can ensure that those influences never outweigh merit.

Because at the end of the day, *the iron doesn't lie*. And neither should we.

The Silent Lesson from a Senior Judge

There are some conversations that stay with you long after the lights fade and the trophies are packed away.

I had the chance to sit alongside one of the most senior judges in Indian bodybuilding. Between two categories, we had the privilege to sip in coffee. Nothing dramatic. Just two judges talking.

I initiated conversation about his past experience and some difficult times of Judging. He looked at the stage, smiled a little, and said, *"You know, over the years, I've had many people from federations approach me. Not directly telling me what to do, but just giving a 'friendly reminder' that this athlete is 'their guy' or 'has a great future."*

He added — ***some judges, especially the newer ones or those chasing a bit of spotlight, they don't stand by their decisions. They'll give scores, then look around to see if it's aligned with the others. If not, they adjust. Just to fit in. Just to please."***

He wasn't bitter when he said it. Just... honest. Calm. Like someone who's seen enough to know how the machine really runs.

He continued, *"Some judges get too carried away trying to stay in favour with the top guys. They listen to the federation heads, nod along, and shift their call quietly. They don't even realise they're compromising — they just think they're playing safe."*

That hit me hard.

Because I've seen it too. The moments where judges second-guess themselves, not because they're unsure about the physique in front of them — but because they're unsure whether their decision will sit well with the power circles behind them.

And that's the real cost of favouritism — it doesn't always come from bad intentions. Sometimes it's born from **fear**, from **insecurity**, from **wanting to belong more than wanting to be right**.

It's a lonely space sometimes — to hold your ground when everyone else leans. To call a show fair when you know someone influential might not like it.

But what this senior judge reminded me is that **our role isn't just to score bodies on a stage. It's to guard the credibility of the sport** — even if that means sitting quietly with your decision while others whisper in corners.

He didn't name names. He didn't gossip. He just said, *"Stand for your call. You don't need to fight every battle, but don't bow to every shadow either."*

It stayed with me.

The Unspoken Ties

Let's be real — the bodybuilding circuit is small. You don't just know the athletes. You know their coaches. You've seen their prep videos. You've maybe done a seminar together, shared dinner post-show, tagged each other in stories.

When you're on the panel, and you know that Trunk No. 18 is coached by a friend of yours — someone who's sitting a few rows away from the stage — it's hard not to feel the pressure.

They might not say a word. They might not ask for any favour. But the awareness of that relationship sits with you. In the back of your mind. Not as an instruction, but as a whisper:

"He's one of ours."
"She's their top girl."
"They've worked hard — don't overlook them."

And even if you're trying to be neutral, that familiarity starts to tug at your decision-making. Not because you're dishonest. But because you're **human**. That's the problem. **Bias doesn't always wear a mask.** Sometimes, it wears a **smile.**

In those moments —you start to realise how thin the line is between **doing what's fair** and **doing what's safe**.

You think:

"If I don't place them well, will they think I did it on purpose?"
"Will this ruin our equation?"
"Will they talk about this backstage, in whispers I'll never hear?"

And this is where the real pressure lives — **in the things left unsaid.**
No one tells you to cheat.
No one hands you a bribe.
No one texts you a list.

No one prepares you for the emotional weight of that seat.

You're handed a scorecard, a pen, and a title — *"Judge."* But what you're really handed… is a moral test.

We all want to believe we're fair. That we judge purely on what we see. That our eyes are loyal only to symmetry, structure, conditioning, presentation.

But the truth?
It's never *just* about the athlete on stage.

There are *stories* standing beside them — stories you know.
There's their coach in the audience.
So what do you do?

These are moments that no rule book prepares you for.

Not the callouts. Not the symmetry checks. Not even the final comparisons.

It's the quiet ones. The moments where your pen hovers above the scorecard, and your thoughts begin to race—not because the decision is unclear, but because the athlete on stage carries a history you know too well. Maybe they're coached by a close friend. Maybe they represent a gym that's been loyal to your federation. Maybe you've watched them rise from amateurs, stumble through seasons, and finally arrive here—desperate for validation.

This is where fairness is tested—not in black and white, but in shades of familiarity.

Philosophers describe moral decision-making in two frames. **Deontology**, where you do what's right regardless of outcome. And **utilitarianism**, where you choose what creates the least harm or the greatest good. Most judges? We live in the grey space between the two. We weigh the rules against relationships, the criteria against consequences, and sometimes, without even realizing it, we bend—not because we're dishonest, but because we're human.

But here's what I've learned sitting in that chair, meet after meet, under spotlight and scrutiny: you cannot serve both fairness and favour.

The stage demands clarity. The athlete deserves truth. And the sport relies on judges who can make tough decisions not because they're cold, but because they care—enough to be consistent, enough to stand alone when needed, and enough to protect the sanctity of the scoreboard.

Because the minute we let familiarity cloud our judgment, we dilute everything we claim to uphold. We reward networks, not physiques.

So what should a judge do?

Be honest—not just with the athletes, but with yourself. Recognize the whispers of bias, no matter how noble they sound. And in that defining moment, choose the athlete who **earned** it, not the one who's **expected** to win.

You may lose a few smiles. You may face some difficult conversations backstage. But what you gain is far more valuable—**credibility**. And once you've built that, athlete by athlete, show by show, it becomes your legacy

And that? That's worth more than any favour.

Being honest isn't hard.

Staying honest without losing your people — that's hard.

Because this sport is built on relationships.

And the moment you choose fairness over familiarity, someone will pull away.

They won't say it.
They'll just stop calling.
Stop inviting.
Stop acknowledging.

And yet, if you choose familiarity over fairness — *you'll lose yourself.*

And that, to me, is the deeper philosophy of judging.

Because at the end of the day, the real winner isn't the one who walks away with the trophy.

It's the judge who walks away with a clean conscience.

Does reputation affect placing?

On paper, no. Judging is about what's on stage that day: symmetry, proportion, conditioning, presentation. The rulebooks don't mention Instagram followers, sponsorships, or how many shows you've won before. The stage resets for every competitor, every show. That's how it's supposed to work.

But in reality? Sometimes reputation walks in before the athlete does.

Let's stop pretending it doesn't. **Yes — reputation *can* affect placing.** I've seen it, I've felt it, and at times, I've even had to fight against its influence in the judging seat.

When a well-known athlete walks on stage, the atmosphere changes. Not just for the crowd — but for the panel too. Maybe they're a defending champion, maybe they're a national icon, or maybe they're coached by someone who's famous in fitness industry. Their presence doesn't just land on stage — it lands in your subconscious.

I remember judging a show where one particular athlete — let's call him *"The Poster Boy"* — was the talk of the show. When he stepped on stage, the crowd erupted before he even hit his first pose.

But here's what no one in the audience saw — he was off. Not majorly. But enough. Soft around the midsection, slightly off conditioned, and his tan had an uneven sheen that distracted from his symmetry.

Now, the dilemma. Right next to him was a lesser-known athlete — newer, quieter, not a fan favorite. But sharp as a blade. Dry, conditioned, tight waist, and near-flawless posing. The kind of physique you'd reward *if* your eyes weren't already clouded by legacy.

In moments like this, reputation becomes noise.

Some judges — consciously or unconsciously — let that noise seep in. They start justifying in their head: *"He's only slightly off,"* or *"He's got that size,", "He's got muscle maturity."*

This is how reputation *can* nudge decisions in close calls. Not because of corruption. But because of comfort. Familiarity creates a psychological bias called the **"halo effect."** You've seen them do well before — so your mind starts connecting dots that may not be there this time.

But here's where maturity kicks in.

An honest judge — a real judge — **knows when to shut the noise out.**

We are not here to clap for your past. We are here to assess your present. This sport, at its core, is about what you bring to the stage *on that day, in that moment*. Your name doesn't get judged — your physique does.

So, does reputation affect placing?

It *does*.

But a good judge doesn't let it.

And a great one?
He makes sure the crowd cheers for *the right athlete* — not just the familiar one.

The Mind Sees What It Already Knows

Let me tell you something that many won't admit, but every experienced judge understands deep down.

Sometimes, without even meaning to, we start judging with our memory instead of our eyes.

You see a Men's Physique line-up. 20 guys on stage. All posing, all shining under the same lights. But your eyes stop on the one you recognize — the guy who won last year, or someone you saw trending on social media, or maybe an athlete trained by a well-known coach. And right there, *before the judging even begins,* your brain has made a connection.

You're not doing it on purpose. But it happens. That little voice in your head goes, *"He's good. He's consistent. He's a champ."*

And that's where we need to be careful.

Because what we're seeing is not just today's physique — we're also seeing yesterday's reputation.

I often say:

"If we could hide every face and name and just look at the bodies — many placing's would change."

And it's true.

The mind loves what it already knows. It's easier to trust a familiar athlete. You feel safe placing them higher. But that's not fair to the new guy, the underdog, the one who came in sharp and ready but isn't known by the crowd — or by the judges.

Now let me be honest — yes, reputation can affect placing *in some panels.* Especially if the judging isn't strong or confident. Some judges get carried away by the crowd's reaction. Others don't want to go against a "big name" athlete. It happens.

But a mature judge? A good judge?

We're not here to reward popularity. We're not here to clap for last year's winner.

We're here to score what's in front of us — right now, under the lights, with no filter.

And that takes focus. That takes honesty.

And sometimes, it takes the courage to place someone *new* ahead of someone *famous.*

Because that's what fairness really means.

Real-world Outcomes that Sparked Debate

Mr. Olympia Controversies

The 1971 Mr. Olympia

The **1971 Mr. Olympia**, held in Paris, was anticipated with tremendous excitement. The stage was set for a historic showdown between the sport's legends: **Sergio Oliva** — "The Myth" — and the **Arnold Schwarzenegger.**

Sergio Oliva, a three-time Mr. Olympia champion and arguably the most genetically gifted bodybuilder of his era, arrived in Paris ready to compete. He was thick, massive, and still considered Arnold's biggest threat.

But days before the show, Sergio was **disqualified by the IFBB** (International Federation of Bodybuilding and Fitness). Why?

Because he had competed in **non-IFBB sanctioned events** earlier that year — specifically, the NABBA Mr. Universe. Back then, the IFBB, under the leadership of Joe Weider, was cracking down on athletes participating in other federations. It was part of a struggle to establish the IFBB as the dominant global federation.

And he wasn't the only one. Several top athletes were barred from competing that year for the same reason, including **Franco Columbu**, leaving only **Arnold Schwarzenegger** to compete... **alone.**

Arnold himself later admitted that this wasn't his proudest moment. He walked out, performed his routine, and accepted the title. But there was **no rivalry, no comparison, no audience roar from a head-to-head battle.**

Just a lone victory that felt more political than physical.

And that's where the **real controversy lies** — not in Arnold winning, but in **why no one else was allowed to compete.**

Was it a fair enforcement of rules?

Or was it a strategic move to clear the way for Arnold's reign?

That question still floats around in bodybuilding circles like a ghost.

The 1981 Mr. Olympia

Franco Columbu, a legend in his own right, returned to the stage after a four-year break. His comeback was nothing short of courageous — especially considering the devastating knee injury he had suffered in 1977 during the World's Strongest Man. But the question that lingers is this: *Was he really in the best shape that day?* Or was it his legacy that stepped on stage, not his physique?

From a judge's perspective, there were technical issues. His upper body still carried that signature Franco density, no doubt. But his lower body told a different story — one of imbalance. His right leg hadn't fully recovered. The quad looked visibly smaller, lacking the sweep and separation we expect at that level. And in bodybuilding, especially at the Olympia, **symmetry and proportion aren't negotiable** — they're pillars of the scoring criteria.

Now, when you place that next to someone like **Tom Platz**, it becomes even harder to justify the decision. Platz brought freakish leg development, razor-sharp conditioning, and a posing routine that had the crowd on fire. He was complete. Another name that often gets overlooked is **Danny Padilla** — one of the most symmetrical and aesthetically balanced athletes of that line-up. His condition, roundness, and flow were exactly what the rulebook preaches.

But despite these stronger contenders, Franco took the title. And here's where it gets complicated. Was it truly about the physique on the stage that night — or did the **weight of his reputation** tip the scale?

This is where the lines blur. It forces us to reflect: Are we judging a moment or a legacy? Are we influenced, even subconsciously, by who the athlete *is*, rather than what they're *presenting*?

And if I've learned anything from sitting on the judging panel, it's this: **Every athlete deserves to be judged for who they are today — not who they were years ago.**

The 1994 Mr. Olympia

At the center of the storm were two titans: **Dorian Yates** and **Shawn Ray**. There are moments when you're not just looking at bodies; you're weighing legacies, expectations, and the very definition of what bodybuilding should reward.

Let's talk about **Dorian** first. He was the face of the "mass monster" era — grainy conditioning, dense muscle maturity, and that freak factor that made jaws drop. But in 1994, he had a torn left bicep. And it showed. The asymmetry was visible — especially in the front double biceps and side chest poses. The shape of his arm was off, and it affected the flow of his otherwise dominating physique.

Now enter **Shawn Ray** — arguably the most aesthetically gifted man on that stage that night. Tight waist, balanced limbs, excellent posing, and flawless conditioning. He was the walking textbook of symmetry, proportion, and presentation. And more importantly — *he was complete.* No injury, no imbalance, no moment where he looked "off."

So the question became: *Do you reward size and legacy, or do you reward balance and perfection?*

This is where the judging seat starts to feel like a moral battleground. The scorecards gave the win to Dorian, and many fans and insiders still question whether that decision was driven by **the fear of breaking the champion's streak** — or by the genuine belief that Dorian's overall mass still outclassed Shawn's perfection.

The 1997 Mr. Olympia

It was **Dorian Yates**, going for his sixth Sandow trophy. By now, Dorian was already a legend. The "Shadow." The man who ushered in an era of grainy density, brutal thickness, and a level of conditioning that changed the benchmark of freakdom. But in 1997 — his physique showed **wear and tear**. His **bicep and triceps injuries** had visibly worsened. His silhouette no longer flowed. From the back, sure, he was still monstrous. But from the front? The symmetry was broken. The lines were blurred.

And then, there was **Nasser El Sonbaty**.

Nasser brought something that night that made the front row lean in and whisper. He was massive, yes — but also full, balanced, and arguably in the best condition of his life. His **front poses**, particularly the **front double biceps and side chest**, looked fuller, rounder, and more aesthetically intact than Dorian's. His presentation had a polished aggression to it — the kind that says, "I came here to take this."

So, what happened?

Despite the murmurs backstage, despite the crowd's roaring preference during comparisons, the title still went to Dorian Yates.

And here's where the controversy lives: Was Dorian really better that night — or was he just "too big to dethrone"

Many felt Nasser had done enough to dethrone Dorian — especially given the **visible muscular injuries** and unbalanced arm shots Dorian presented. But the judges leaned toward **conditioning, density, and reputation** — perhaps giving Dorian the benefit of the doubt one last time.

And for many fans, that decision — quiet and clinical as it looked on the scorecards — left a loud echo that still vibrates through bodybuilding history.

The 2001 Mr. Olympia

This is by far my favourite battle.

Ronnie Coleman, the reigning champ, came into the show chasing his *fourth* consecutive Mr. Olympia title. By then, Ronnie was already a mass monster — famous for his otherworldly size, alien-like muscle bellies, and a freak factor that made audiences gasp the moment he walked out.

But in **2001**, something felt different. Ronnie's conditioning was slightly off — especially in the **midsection**. His usual granite look appeared a bit **watery** in certain poses, and his **abdominal control** was a recurring concern.

Then came **Jay Cutler** — younger, fresher, and **sharpened like a blade**. His conditioning was on point. Bone dry. His waist was tighter, his quads were sliced, and his presentation screamed, *"It's my time."* His **front shots** were particularly impressive, and when the comparisons started — the crowd **sided with Jay**. Loudly.

Judges, however, did not.

Ronnie Coleman still walked away with the **Sandow**, and Jay took second — but the margin was thin. Very thin. Because many believed Jay had **actually beaten Ronnie** — at least *that night*. His physique was arguably better conditioned, better balanced, and better presented.

Jay didn't walk away bitter. Instead, he walked away *motivated*. That night *planted the seed* for one of the most iconic rivalries in bodybuilding history. Jay kept coming back — year after year — and eventually took the title in **2006**, dethroning Ronnie and cementing his own legacy.

The 2007 Mr. Olympia

Jay Cutler came into 2007 as the reigning Mr. Olympia after finally dethroning Ronnie Coleman the previous year in 2006. That was a landmark win — Jay had been chasing that Sandow for years and had finally taken down the king. But winning is one thing... defending the title is another.

Enters **Victor Martinez** — Dominican pride, incredible structure, flowing lines, and crisp conditioning. In 2007, Victor showed up **arguably at his all-time best**. He had that **small waist, round muscle bellies, and deep cuts** — especially in his quads and abs. His **posing was clean**, confident, and every time he hit a side chest, you could feel the tension in the arena.

Now contrast that with **Jay**, who came in **big and full**, but clearly **off in conditioning**. His midsection was blurry, his hamstrings lacked the separation fans had come to expect, and his overall look lacked the wow factor he had when he beat Ronnie.

So when they stood side by side... the question buzzed in every corner of the Orleans Arena. Because to many — including long-time fans and even some seasoned pros — **Victor Martinez looked like the winner**.

Jay had the mass, sure, but that alone wasn't enough this time. The audience reaction said it all. There were **boos** when Jay was announced as the winner. Not because people hated him — but because they **felt robbed** of what looked like a moment of truth for Victor.

It also taught us that **fans don't forget** when someone gets too close and doesn't get the win. Victor's missed moment still stings in many circles. And Jay? He proved his doubters wrong by showing up shredded in 2009 to reclaim the title.

The 2014 Mr. Olympia

The 50th anniversary of the Mr. Olympia was supposed to be a grand celebration — the pinnacle of bodybuilding's legacy. But what unfolded on that Las Vegas stage became one of the most debated results in modern Olympia history.

This was the year the rivalry between **Phil Heath** and **Kai Greene** reached its boiling point — not just physically, but emotionally, theatrically, and publicly. The two had been the top two in 2012 and 2013, but in 2014, it became personal. And when bodybuilding gets personal, objectivity often gets clouded — not by the judges, but by the audience, the fans, and even the media.

From the first comparisons, it was clear — this was a two-man show. The other competitors, despite world-class physiques, were simply not in the same league that night.

- **Phil Heath** stepped in with his signature round muscle bellies, deep separation, and unmatched fullness. His delts, arms, and overall density were textbook Olympia.
- **Kai Greene**, on the other hand, was sharper. His conditioning was better in many eyes. His legs were more detailed, and his posing — artistic and fluid — resonated with the crowd.

But this wasn't just a physical battle. It was emotional warfare. At one point, they nearly touched foreheads. The moment was tense, unscripted, and real.

By finals, Kai looked slightly tighter. His posing routine brought the house down with a performance that blended grace, intensity, and storytelling. Phil's routine, in contrast, was less theatrical but structurally solid, hitting every mandatory shot with confidence.

The crowd's reaction leaned toward Kai — not just because of his performance, but possibly because he was seen as the underdog, the emotional choice.

The official scorecard revealed the following:

- **Phil Heath**
  - Prejudging: 5 points
  - Finals: 5 points
  - Total: 10 points
- **Kai Greene**
  - Prejudging: 10 points
  - Finals: 10 points
  - Total: 20 points

In IFBB scoring, the lower the score, the better the placement. Phil won both rounds with unanimous firsts, which technically leaves little room for argument. But bodybuilding judging isn't as simple as numbers — because physiques are not numbers.

So why did this result cause such an uproar?

1. **Fan Perception vs. Scoring Sheet**: To the audience, Kai brought more emotion, better conditioning, and a more compelling performance. Phil brought balance, proportion, and dominant muscle density. The disagreement was less about who was better, and more about *what* defines "better."
2. **Rivalry and Narrative**: Kai Greene was the anti-hero in this story — self-made, artistic, less commercial. Phil Heath, the reigning champ, represented establishment. For many, rooting for Kai was rooting for raw passion over polished status.
3. **Scorecard Discrepancy**: The scorecard showed Phil with unanimous wins, which led some fans to question: *How could it be that clear-cut when the physiques were so closely matched?* This fed into speculation, even conspiracy, though there was no concrete evidence of manipulation.

Phil Heath walked away with his fourth Sandow, continuing his dynasty. But many walked away from the venue believing they had witnessed a different kind of winner.

The 2018 Mr. Olympia

The 2018 Mr. Olympia was set to be history in the making — **Phil Heath** was aiming for his **eighth consecutive title**, which would tie the all-time record held by **Ronnie Coleman** and **Lee Haney**. Phil Heath had been dominant from 2011 to 2017. His combination of round muscle bellies, razor-sharp symmetry, and dense proportions was hard to beat. Even in years when his conditioning wasn't perfect, his structure often carried him through.

Most notably, Phil had undergone **hernia surgery in 2017**, and his midsection — often a point of critique — had become a central topic of conversation. Would he be able to tighten it? Would he come in sharp enough? The questions were there, and everyone was watching.

Shawn Rhoden, known for his aesthetics, flowing lines, and calm stage presence, had been a consistent top-tier athlete. But few saw him as the one to dethrone Phil.

In 2018, however, he came in with something different — **crisp conditioning, paper-thin skin, tight midsection, and symmetry that harkened back to the golden era.**

He wasn't the biggest man on stage — far from it — but he brought a balance that demanded attention.

From the first callouts, the energy was different.

- Phil appeared full and dense, but his **midsection looked distended** — especially in relaxed poses and transitions.
- Shawn, on the other hand, hit every pose with **sharp lines, a tight waist, and controlled breathing**. His abdominal-thigh pose and front double biceps were clean and polished.

The crowd reaction told a story — it was the first time in years that a real challenger looked like he *might* be ahead of the reigning champ.

Shawn's posing was deliberate and fluid. He didn't just hit poses — he presented them. His transitions were clean, and he stayed composed.

Phil's posing, though confident, didn't seem to silence the critiques about his waist.

When the final comparisons happened, it was clear that **conditioning vs. size** was at play — and in 2018, conditioning won.

Official Scorecard:

Round	Shawn Rhoden	Phil Heath
Prejudging	7	8
Finals	6	9
Total	**13**	**17**

Shawn Rhoden won both rounds unanimously from the judging panel.

Was It Controversial?

1. **Phil's Legacy and Expectations**: The controversy wasn't just about physiques — it was about **legacy**. Many fans were emotionally invested in seeing Phil match Coleman and Haney's record. The loss felt like a shock, especially since many believed he wasn't "off" enough to lose.
2. **Conditioning vs. Mass Debate**: This result reaffirmed an important shift — **conditioning and aesthetics** can outweigh pure size. Some fans believed Shawn was too small to win an Olympia. Others argued he represented a return to classical ideals.
3. **Fan Division**: Bodybuilding fans are passionate — and divided. Some argued that **Phil still had the better physique overall** and should have won despite the midsection. Others celebrated **Shawn's clean lines** and saw the result as justice for aesthetics.

Whether you agreed with the decision or not, 2018 was a landmark moment. It signalled that aesthetic presentation and conditioning could dethrone mass and dominance.

The Delhi Storm: Ali Bilal vs. Bhuwan Chauhan

– *When the Crowd Saw One Thing, and the Judges Saw Another*

There are shows you attend… and then there are shows you remember. The 2023 IHFF Sheru Classic Pro Show in Delhi? That one falls in the second category for me.

Not because of the lighting or the crowd or the noise—though all of that was there. It was because of what happened *after* the winner was announced. I've been around this sport long enough to know when a result is going to stir the pot. And this one? The pot wasn't just stirred. It was boiling.

Ali Bilal came out looking sharp—his physique was tight, aesthetic, and honestly, in some poses, it was hard to find a flaw. Wide clavicles, deep chest, clean abs, unmatchable obliques, and full muscle bellies. He looked like someone who had done his homework. A lot of people in the audience had only one reaction when he walked out: *"He's winning this."*

Bhuwan Chauhan, on the other hand, brought his usual game—Structure, experience, and confidence. The guy knows how to command the stage. He's been around, and that experience shows. Rahul Paswan was right in the mix too—great shape, quality mass, superb structure, and very composed.

But when the final results were announced—Bhuwan 1st, Rahul 2nd, Ali Bilal 3rd—you could feel it. The crowd didn't react with celebration. They reacted with confusion. Some were genuinely angry. Not because they had anything against Bhuwan or Rahul, but because Ali looked *that* good. He had ticked every box.

After the show, it was all anyone was talking about—coaches, athletes, even casual fans on social media. Side-by-side comparisons started showing up on stories. Posing breakdowns were being made within hours. I even had a few people call me just to ask, "Bro, did you see Ali's front pose? How did that not win?"

And look—It's not easy. You're not judging a photo on Instagram. You're watching five to eight guys on stage, under lights, sometimes from a tricky angle, all hitting the same pose. And in those 60-90 seconds, you have to assess who presents the *complete* package: balance, flow, conditioning, presentation, and structure.

The more I saw the social media debates heat up, the more restless I became — not because I wanted to pick sides, but because, as a judge myself, I was consumed by this need to understand what the panel *really saw* that day. When you watch the clips online, frame by frame, you get caught up in isolated moments — a better back shot here, a more confident transition. But live judging isn't about snapshots. It's about flow, presence, and the cumulative impression an athlete makes across multiple rounds. Still, I kept thinking — *what if I was on that panel? Would I have scored it differently? Or would I have seen what they saw?* That's the thing about this role — even when you're not judging a show, your brain doesn't switch off.

I remember wishing—almost desperately—that I had the number of the head judge at that moment, just to call and ask, "What was the thought process behind the final placing?" Not out of frustration, not to challenge their authority, but purely out of curiosity and a deep desire to understand better.

When Ali secured second place at the 2024 Olympia, it was a moment that made you stop and think. It wasn't just about his standing in the competition, but the journey that led to it. He didn't let the surrounding controversy overshadow his focus. His back, which had been a point of discussion in previous shows, was more developed and balanced. His conditioning was on point, and his stage presence was mesmerizing. It was the kind of performance that had the audience and judges taking notice. His transition from that controversial IHFF show to Olympia was nothing short of remarkable.

Too Big for the Board shorts

It was during a national-level show. Arvind, a well-known figure with a loyal fan base, walked out with immense confidence. His physique was dense, thick, and powerful — his lats flared out wide, arms full, and muscle density that spoke of countless hours of hard core training.

And then, right there, in front of everyone — a comment came from the judging panel: *"Your physique doesn't suit the Men's Physique category. You should consider switching to Bodybuilding."* Not because he wasn't good — but because he was too developed for the category. His size, muscularity, and overall structure aligned far more with Classic or even Open Bodybuilding. In Men's Physique, the judging focuses on balance, aesthetic flow, and upper-body dominance with beach-body symmetry — not deep muscle separation or extreme size.

This wasn't a dismissal — it was a redirection. A tough pill, no doubt. For an athlete who had prepped for months, with his mind fixed on the Men's Physique title, it felt like a rejection. And this is where the sport tests not just your muscles, but your mindset. Arvind could've taken it personally, but instead, he took it as a challenge. In the months that followed, he began reshaping his presentation, refining his posing, and channelling his physique toward a category that would embrace his density — Classic Bodybuilding.

And in a few months, **he came back stronger — securing his IFBB Pro Card in the Classic Physique division.** The same muscle that made him "too much" for one division became his weapon in another.

That moment — once awkward, even controversial — became a **Launchpad**. It's a lesson for every athlete: Sometimes when they say, *"You don't belong here,"* they're not rejecting you. They're telling you that you're meant for something bigger. **Every category isn't for everyone**. And as judges, it's our job not just to award physiques — but to help guide athletes toward where their true potential lies. Not out of bias, not out of favouritism — but out of respect for the sport, and for the athlete's own long-term success.

This moment wasn't just about Arvind — it was a reflection of what many athletes face when their progress begins to clash with category guidelines. It’s tough. Do you hold back development to stay relevant in a division? Or do you evolve into the next stage of the sport?

Part III
Beyond the Stage

The Business of Bodybuilding

Competing vs. profiting: What's the real ROI?

Let's clear something up — **there's no money in winning shows.** Not in the kind of money that justifies what you spend to get there.

Most shows won't give you more than a medal, a plastic trophy, maybe a small cash prize if you're lucky, and a few photos that circulate online for a few days. That's it. The stage won't pay your bills. Prep expenses, coaching, travel, tan, diet, time off work — you'll always spend more than you earn.

An athlete may spend **lakhs** excluding meal expenses per show. And most walk away with **a medal, a stage photo, and experience**, not a cheque.

So then why do it?

Because the **real money isn't in the win — it's in how you use it.** You don't get paid for being muscular. You get paid for being **marketable**.

What people really pay for is your **persona**, your **presence**, your **energy**, and your ability to **communicate value**. You become profitable the moment you turn yourself into a **personal brand** —

when people don't just look at your body, they listen to your voice. They trust your advice. They follow your process. They want to learn from you, train with you, and collaborate with you.

That's when things start shifting:

- Brands approach you not just for your shape — but because you **fit their image.**
- Clients sign up with you not just for your results — but because of **how you carry yourself.**
- You get invited to speak, coach, host, judge — not because of one win, but because people remember you.

And all of this doesn't happen **after** the show — it starts **before** it. In how you document your prep, how you speak on camera, how you engage on social media, how you respect the sport and represent yourself like a professional — long before your name is called on stage.

So yes, compete. Bring your best. Chase that medal if it fuels you. But if you want to **make a life out of this**, don't just train your body — **build your presence.**

Because at the end of the day, **you are the brand**, not the trophy.

Sponsorships, endorsements, and influence

Sponsorships and brand endorsements don't always chase the champion. They chase *influence*. And influence is built through authenticity, storytelling, and consistent connection with an audience. Look at someone like **Simeon Panda** – he built his legacy through consistency, branding and visual excellence Or **Chris Bumstead (CBum)** — yes, he's a multiple-time Classic Physique Mr. Olympia, but his brand is worth far more than just his trophies. His openness about anxiety, training style, and behind-the-scenes vlogs made him a household name, well beyond bodybuilding fans.

What Brands Actually Want

It's easy to think sponsorships come when you hit a certain level of leanness or muscularity. But brands don't care only about your abs. They care about:

- **Audience Engagement**: Do people respond to you? Do they comment, share, repost, or trust your voice?
- **Communication Skills**: Can you promote a product naturally? Can you talk on camera without sounding forced?
- **Lifestyle Alignment**: Do your values and content reflect the brand's image?
- **Consistency**: Are you reliable with content? Do you show up, post, train, and represent regularly?

This is why many pros — even Olympia-level athletes — struggle to land long-term deals. Meanwhile, some amateurs or lifestyle influencers are signing six-figure contracts because they understand **the business of influence**.

Take **Jeremy Buendia** — a multiple-time Men's Physique Olympia champ. In spite of taking a break, his social media presence, courses, training plans, and supplement endorsements helped him sustain his income. His followers didn't vanish when he left the stage — because his *brand* didn't rely solely on his placings.

Sponsorships vs. Endorsements vs. Affiliations

Here's what many athletes confuse:

- **Sponsorships**: You are paid or supported to represent a brand (often includes salary, travel, product, exposure).
- **Endorsements**: You publicly support or promote a product, sometimes on a one-time or contract basis.
- **Affiliate Marketing**: You earn commission for sales through your link/code. No salary, but passive potential.

Many newer athletes sign up as "sponsored" but are actually affiliates — no base pay, only commission. There's nothing wrong with that — but it's important to understand where you stand and how you want to grow.

What It Takes to Get Sponsored

- **Create Your Niche**: Are you the hard-working underdog? The science-based lifter? The comic relief in the gym? The glam fitness queen? Define it. Own it.
- **Be Active Across Platforms**: Instagram alone isn't enough anymore. YouTube, TikTok, podcasts, and even Twitter (X) can expand your brand reach.
- **Professionalism in Approach**: Draft a portfolio. Treat sponsorship pitches like job applications. Include stats, photos, engagement insights, and your vision.
- **Consistency in Content**: Show your life, not just your flex. People connect with your dog, your diet, your off days, your values.

Many athletes seek for sponsorships too early. My advice: **build first, attract later.** Sponsors come to those who are already moving — already growing.

I've seen it too often — an athlete places top 3 in a regional show and starts cold-emailing ten supplement companies. But they've got 1,200 followers, no consistent content, and no message. That's not how this works. Instead, build a *community* — even if it's just 500 loyal people. Make content that teaches, inspires, or entertains. Let your work speak, and the sponsors will find you.

In today's bodybuilding business, your physique may get you noticed — but your **influence** is what gets you paid.

The Dark Side: Profit vs. Purpose

At the heart of every bodybuilding competition is the balance between **revenue** and **expenses**. From entry fees to sponsorships, several income streams fuel the financial machinery.

Revenue Streams

- **Entry Fees**: Athletes pay fees to compete, which vary based on the event's prestige. These fees range from **₹5,000 to ₹35,000**, depending on the category and event level.
- **Ticket Sales**: Big Shows often generate revenue by selling tickets to spectators. With prices ranging from **₹300** to **₹500.**
- **Expo Booth Rentals**: Companies, ranging from supplement brands to fitness equipment manufacturers, pay to rent booths at bodybuilding expos. The cost for these booths can go anywhere from **₹25,000 to ₹10,00,000**, depending on the size, location and visibility.
- **Sponsorships**: Corporate sponsors are a critical income source for most bodybuilding events. Major supplement brands, clothing lines, and other fitness-related companies enter into lucrative sponsorship deals with show organizers. These sponsorships can bring in **₹5,00,000 to several lakhs** depending on the scale of the event.

Costs of Running a Show

- **Venue Costs**: Renting a venue is one of the largest expenses for an organizer. The cost can range from **₹3–20 lakhs** or more depending on the size, venue, and date of the show.
- **Logistics**: Event organizers must cover everything from backstage operations, tanning services, photographers, and medical teams. This also includes the logistics of transporting the equipment and setting up the event space.

- **Marketing**: Promoting a bodybuilding show involves significant advertising expenses. A well-targeted marketing campaign can cost anywhere from **₹50,000 to ₹2,00,000** per month depending on the medium used.

This is where bodybuilding enters murky waters. As the industry grows more lucrative, there are times when the original spirit of the sport—dedication, discipline, and fair competition—starts to get eclipsed by commercial motives.

- **Category Inflation:** To increase participation (and revenue), federations sometimes introduce numerous sub-divisions with minimal differentiation. This results in watered-down competition and unclear judging criteria.
- **Stage Time vs. Entry Volume:** More entries mean more income—but often at the cost of athlete experience. Athletes may get rushed stage time, chaotic backstage logistics, or poorly managed callouts.
- **Favouritism through Sponsorship Influence:** If an athlete is backed by a major brand or event sponsor, there can be an unconscious (or intentional) bias. Their presence might command indirect influence on scores.
- **Unfiltered Entries:** Organizers may avoid enforcing strict entry requirements in terms of conditioning or prep levels. More athletes equals more revenue, even if some aren't truly stage-ready.
- **Backstage Neglect:** With the event maximized for business, athlete care often takes a backseat. Poor facilities, lack of coordination, rushed tanning or pumping areas, and no time for adequate posing preparation.
- **Commercial Exploitation of Data:** Athlete registrations are goldmines. Emails, contact info, supplement usage patterns—all these are often used for remarketing or passed on to sponsors without clear consent.

All of this raises a simple but critical question: is the athlete truly the priority?

Profit and purpose can co-exist—but only if the people involved actively choose to prioritize fairness, professionalism, and the long-term credibility of the sport.

Where the Iron Divides: Federation Identity and Influence

There was a time when bodybuilding meant one single federation, one unified goal: building the ultimate human physique. But as the sport grew, so did its branches. Multiple federations emerged—each with its own standards, judging guidelines, athlete grooming rules, and most importantly, its own **agenda.**

Some federations prided themselves on discipline and old-school structure. Others leaned toward glamour and accessibility. Some focused on international reach; others guarded their local turf like loyal kingdoms. For the athlete, this created choices—but also confusion. Do you choose the federation that has better shows? Or the one where your coach sits on the judging panel? Or the one that gives faster pro cards, easier wins, and louder social media presence?

Suddenly, what should have been a sport about **merit** became a game of **alignment.**

Let's be honest—most athletes don't read the judging rulebook. They learn from what gets rewarded. And what gets rewarded is often a reflection of **the federation's culture.** In some federations, a full chest and razor-sharp conditioning might dominate. In others, it's the athlete with a larger social media presence or the right affiliations who earns the top spot.

And the deeper you go, the more you see how federations function almost like tribes. Each has its **star players, inner circles,** and unspoken codes of loyalty. These aren't written anywhere—but if you know, you know.

For a new athlete, this division can be overwhelming. You're told to "just focus on your physique," but the truth is more complicated. You might step onstage at one federation and get first place, only to switch federations and not even make top five.

Did your physique change overnight? Or did the standards—and expectations—change?

This is not corruption. This is **subjectivity with a structure.** Every federation has the right to protect its brand. But athletes often pay the price—forced to modify their bodies not just for progress, but for compatibility with federation tastes. That's not growth. That's **adaptation under pressure.**

Judging should be the last neutral ground. But even this realm can become a battlefield of interests. Judges might belong to one federation but also coach in another. Or they may be influenced by personal loyalties, regional alliances, or past backstage stories. Some federations promote judges who toe the political line. Others lose great judges because they refuse to play along.

In India, many federations operate on a regional level, often with little to no connection to international bodies. This decentralization has led to **a fragmented system** where rules, judging criteria, and even the very essence of the sport can change from one show to the next. The result is a muddled environment where **clarity is sacrificed for convenience.**

A common scenario, especially in regional or national shows, is the presence of officials who are either ex-players, old-school coaches, or individuals who have been given a spot out of respect—**but not necessarily because they have the qualifications or understanding of modern bodybuilding standards**. In fact, if you were to ask these officials about the criteria for different divisions, the responses would vary widely. Some would talk about the "good old days," while others might throw in buzzwords that reflect more about their personal biases than any concrete, objective standard.

When you have judges who have never actually read the guidelines for their specific federation—let alone understood the science and aesthetics behind modern bodybuilding criteria—**it's a recipe for confusion.** The landscape is littered with inconsistencies. Athletes show up, work hard to prepare, and get judged based on who knows what.

For example, in some federations, an emphasis might be placed on size over conditioning, while in others, symmetry and aesthetics take precedence. To make matters worse, the feedback athletes get often sounds more like personal opinions rather than constructive, standardized critique. This discrepancy becomes especially clear when athletes move between federations. A bodybuilder who wins in one federation might barely place in another, not because their physique has changed, but because the **criteria have shifted** under the whims of the judging panel.

Perhaps the most concerning aspect of the current system is the absence of formal education and training for those sitting at the judging table. Many officials in India come from a legacy of being respected players in the sport or have a rich history in coaching. However, as time passes, bodybuilding evolves, and judging must adapt to those changes. The fact that many officials **have never read the guidelines**—much less comprehended the advanced methodologies behind modern bodybuilding—creates a massive void.

For Indian bodybuilding to truly mature and elevate itself, the issue of education must be addressed at every level. It's not enough for officials to have "experience"; they need to have **trained eyes and knowledge**. Judging panels should be made up of people who not only know bodybuilding from the inside out but also understand the evolving standards set by **international federations**.

Additionally, there needs to be an overhaul of how athletes are briefed on judging criteria and how those criteria are consistently implemented. Until then, athletes may continue to feel frustrated with the lack of transparency and fairness in the process.

Federations will continue to rise, clash, and evolve. But the athletes deserve a system that rewards honesty over affiliation, consistency over convenience. Judges deserve the freedom to decide without whispers in their ears. And the sport, at its heart, deserves **a united soul.**

The Coach-Athlete Dynamic

In the world of bodybuilding, the relationship between coaches and athletes is one of the most crucial dynamics, often determining the success or failure of a career. Coaches are seen as mentors, guides, and experts, helping athletes navigate the rigorous world of training, diet, and competition. However, beneath the surface, this dynamic is not always as clear-cut. The fine line between mentorship and exploitation is frequently blurred, and many athletes find themselves caught in relationships that may not always serve their best interests. Some coaches play a critical role in fostering growth, while others may manipulate and control their athletes, pushing them beyond their limits for personal gain.

In the ideal scenario, a coach is someone who nurtures an athlete's potential, guiding them through the intricacies of bodybuilding training and competition. They offer advice on training regimens, diet plans, and mental preparation. The best coaches understand that bodybuilding is not just about muscle size and strength, but also about the mental fortitude to withstand the pressure, the discipline to push through physical pain, and the emotional resilience required to excel. They create a supportive environment where athletes feel encouraged to reach their full potential, not just physically but mentally and emotionally as well.

However, the dark side of coaching exists when a coach begins to exert too much control, turning the relationship from mentorship into exploitation. This occurs when a coach becomes more focused on their own gain—whether that be financial, personal, or professional—at the expense of the athlete's well-being. Athletes, particularly young or inexperienced ones, can become overly reliant on their coaches, sometimes to the point of blind dependence. They may trust their coach's guidance unquestioningly, even when it contradicts their personal instincts or needs.

The Talent Trap – When Genetics Become a Business

I've seen it happen so many times, it's almost predictable now.

An athlete steps on stage for maybe their first or second show. Young, fresh, maybe even a little unsure of their poses. But the moment they hit a shot—bam—you know they're different. Their body just *works*. Great structure, small waist, round muscles. It's clear—they're a genetic freak.

And you can bet the moment they step off stage, their phone starts buzzing.

Some coaches adopt a strategic approach where they offer free training to genetically gifted athletes, or "genetic freaks," as a way to build their reputation and brand while charging other clients. Now, this isn't just about being generous; it's a smart business move. When a coach works with someone who already has the potential to shine, it makes the coach look like they're the reason for their success. But let's be clear: this strategy isn't about passion for the sport or the athlete; it's about business, optics, and exploiting the marketing power of a naturally gifted individual.

Some often **paying** the athlete to be a part of their team. All because they saw potential.

It might seem like a great deal—free coaching, more exposure on social media, and possibly even opportunities to travel and collab with big names. However, what many might not realize is that it's not always just about helping the athlete; it's also about the coach building their own brand. Coaches understand that they're judged by their results. While the hard work they put in behind the scenes often goes unnoticed, what people focus on are the winners. And athletes with exceptional natural talent are perfect for showcasing success.

In this strategy, the coach may offer free training to those who already have the genetic potential to succeed, using their success as a way to boost their own reputation. At the same time, they charge other clients who are working hard to improve, benefiting from their broader exposure. It's a smart business move, one that highlights the coach's ability to work with top athletes. However, it's important to recognize that the focus is often as much on the coach's brand-building as it is on the athlete's development.

It's not always about coaching skill—it's about who can sign the most genetically gifted people. And that's where things get messy.

Because the truth is—**free coaching usually comes with strings.** Maybe not right away, but it shows up. You might be expected to tag the coach in every post. You might feel forced to compete more often than you planned. You might get pushed harder than your body can handle because they want results *now*, not later.

And if you don't win? If you pull out of a show? If you decide to go another direction? Suddenly that love and support disappears. I've seen athletes get dropped overnight—just because they stopped being useful for the coach's image.

If you're one of those athletes with great genetics, I get it. You'll get attention. People will message you. You'll get offers. And that's not your fault. You earned that spotlight. But just know what you're walking into.

Don't let the hype fool you. Don't jump into the first offer just because it sounds good. Ask questions. See who's really there to help you grow—and who's just trying to grow their own brand.

Because once you're in, it's hard to walk away. And sometimes, the coach who actually charges you, who doesn't care about your followers, who teaches you from the ground up—that's the one who'll really build you.

And if you're the kind of athlete who doesn't get the DMs, who doesn't have the flashy look yet, but you're grinding day in and day out. You're not less. You're not behind. You're just taking the longer path. And the longer path might not be shiny, but it's solid. It's real. You'll earn every inch. And when you finally stand up there and win, it won't be luck or genetics. It'll be because you built it brick by brick.

This industry runs on results. But real results—lasting ones—don't come from shortcuts or hype. They come from time, patience, and the right kind of guidance.

So if you're reading this and you're in that space right now—being pulled by big offers, wondering who to trust—just slow down and ask yourself:

Are they choosing me for me? Or for what I can do for them?

Because there's a big difference between being *valued* and being *used.*

When Loyalty Loses to Spotlight

There are coaches in this sport who truly treat their athletes like family.

They don't just send macros and training plans. They check in when you're quiet. They call you on bad days. They adjust your prep not because it looks good on paper—but because they actually care how you feel.

They'll stay up late analyzing your posing videos. They'll drive hours just to be at your show. They'll pull money from their own pocket to help you get to a national qualifier or cover your tan. Not for clout. Not for followers. Just because they believe in you.

But even those coaches, the real ones, sometimes get left behind.

Because somewhere down the line—when the athlete starts making noise, starts winning, starts catching attention—the offers come in. Big names. Flashy teams. Promises of exposure. High-end photoshoots. Brand connections. A chance to stand beside IFBB pros-and just like that, the athlete walks away.

It's easy to judge and say, "They weren't loyal." But the truth is more complex.

At the core of it, most athletes—especially those with potential—are hungry to be *seen*. To matter. To belong to something that feels elite. It's not always about the plan or the knowledge. It's about the *feeling* of being part of a winning team. That sense of validation.

They start thinking:

- "Maybe I'll grow faster with this new coach."
- "Everyone in that team is winning. I want to be there too."
- "If I stay where I am, people will think I'm not serious."

Social media makes it worse. Athletes compare. They watch others getting reposted, followed, and praised. And even if their current coach is doing everything right, silently, with love and care—it doesn't *look* big enough online.

And the sad truth is: In this sport, visibility often feels more important than loyalty.

So the question comes: Should these coaches stop helping?

It's tempting to say yes. After all, why pour your heart into someone if they might leave the second they get noticed? Why give and give, only to feel discarded when the shine wears off?

But here's the thing…

You don't coach because of loyalty. You coach because that's who you are. Because when someone is lost, you want to guide them. Because when someone believes in themselves for the first time, it gives *you* purpose too.

Yes, some will leave. Yes, it will hurt. But not everyone will forget.

Some will remember your sacrifices. Some will stay. Some will come back, wiser.

And even if they don't—your impact doesn't disappear. It becomes part of their foundation. Whether they say it or not, *they know who helped them when no one else would.*

One thing that needs to be considered here is that the industry rewards visibility, not always authenticity. Coaches who market better, who showcase results, who run big teams—they get more eyes. And that's not necessarily wrong. They've built a system, and some athletes thrive in that setup.

But that doesn't mean your way—quiet, one-on-one, deeply personal—is wrong either.

There's a place for both.

Not every athlete wants to be a brand. Some still want to be seen as a person. And when they find you—the coach who listens, who adjusts plans based on feelings, not followers—they'll stay. Or they'll return. Or they'll tell others about you.

Because while flashy coaches might win attention, you're the one who helps them win stability, mindset, and belief in themselves.

So please don't stop being you. Don't stop helping. But protect your energy. Learn to see the signs. Set boundaries. Coach with love, but don't lose yourself in someone else's dream. Your value isn't based on how many medals your team wins—it's in how many lives you've shaped quietly, without the need for applause.

Not everyone will be loyal. Not every journey ends with a reunion. But your standard—*your integrity—must not change based on someone else's decision.*

Respecting the Athlete, Understanding the Sport

At the end of the day, this sport is built on bodies—but it survives on *people*. Behind every physique is a mind, a heart, a struggle. A story you haven't read. As coaches, judges, spectators, and even fellow athletes—we owe it to the sport to respect that.

Respecting the athlete means more than clapping after their routine. It means understanding their journey. Knowing that even the one who placed last might've overcome more than the one who won gold. That everybody on that stage has been sculpted by sacrifice, shaped by discipline, and fueled by hope.

But it also means telling the truth.

If you're a coach, it's not your job to promise dreams—you guide, you teach, you prepare. But you also tell them when they're not ready. You say what they *need* to hear, not just what they *want* to hear. That's real respect.

And understanding the sport? That means seeing beyond placings and popularity. It means knowing that bodybuilding is not just about who's the biggest or leanest. It's about balance, flow, presence, and poise. It's about showing what's been earned, not just what's been gifted by genetics.

Acknowledging the dedication behind the physique

In bodybuilding, it's easy to get caught up in the final look—the shredded abs, the paper-thin skin, the striated delts under bright lights. But when you truly sit with the sport, when you've judged enough shows and seen enough preps unfold, you start to realize something deeper: the physique is only the tip of the iceberg. What lies beneath is pain, sacrifice, obsession, and an insane level of discipline that most people will never understand.

It was Arnold Schwarzenegger who said, "The resistance that you fight physically in the gym and the resistance that you fight in life can only build a strong character." That quote captures the essence of what every true athlete endures. Because that physique—the one people admire on Instagram or cheer for at a show—is built in moments when no one's watching.

And then there's Ronnie Coleman—eight-time Mr. Olympia and one of the most powerful physiques the world has ever seen. But today, Ronnie walks with crutches and has undergone multiple surgeries on his back and hips. When asked if he regrets the brutal training that led to those injuries, he simply says, "I loved every minute of it. I wouldn't change a thing." That's the mindset of a champion. The willingness to push beyond limits for something you believe in, something you love.

One evening, I got a call from a coach I've known for couple of years now. The kind of guy who doesn't make a lot of noise online, doesn't flex in every post, doesn't go after every trend. Just a humble, hardworking coach with a small gym.

That night, his voice was different. Tired. Disappointed.

He didn't say hello like he usually did. He just sighed and said, **"Sir... I don't know why I'm doing this anymore."**

I asked him what happened.

He said one of his best athletes had just left him. A young men's physique guy—good genetics, very hardworking, great potential. He wasn't always that way though. When he first came in, he was just a quiet kid with big dreams.

This coach built him from scratch.

He stood by him in the off-season, through injuries, through self-doubt. They trained like brothers. He believed in that kid like he was family.

But now? Just a few weeks before a national-level show, the athlete joined a bigger team.

The kind that offers professional media and "inside access" to the big leagues.

No explanation. Just a glossy Instagram post:

"Proud to be joining Coach ______ and taking things to the next level!"

I could hear the heartbreak in his voice when he said, **"After everything I did for him… I didn't even get a call. Not even a thank you. Maybe I'm not meant for this anymore."**

I let him talk. Then I told him this:

"You didn't fail him. You built him. And yeah, he left—but that doesn't erase the work you put in. That doesn't take away the fact that you turned a boy into a stage-ready athlete. That's your gift. And somewhere out there, there's another kid. Another raw talent who's still invisible. And you're the one who's going to find him. Or better yet—you'll help him find *himself*."

He went quiet. Then finally, he laughed a little and said, "You really think I'll come across another one like that?"

I said,

"You won't just find one. You'll *create* one. Again. And again. Because that's what you do."

Because behind every big-name athlete, there's usually a coach who never got the spotlight.

A coach who gave more than he got.

Who loved this sport for the purity of it—before the sponsorships and spotlight ever came into the picture.

To all those coaches out there who feel like giving up because someone left or forgot them—**don't**.

You're not forgotten.

You're just not trending.

And trust me—**you don't need to be popular to be powerful** in someone's life.

Somewhere out there, there's another young man walking into a gym for the first time.

And he's praying to find someone like *you*.

Dorian Yates, the six-time Mr. Olympia, trained in solitude in his dungeon-style gym in Birmingham. He didn't believe in being flashy. He believed in being consistent. He said, "The difference between a good physique and a great one is attention to detail. Every meal, every rep, every hour of sleep counts." That kind of obsession is what separates the elite from the average. And it's not glamorous. It's not fun. But it's real.

We, as judges, spectators, coaches, and fellow athletes, must remember this: not all victories are visible. The athlete who came in tenth might have overcome more than the one who placed first. The man who looked slightly off may have dieted through heartbreak. The woman who missed her peak may have balanced prep with motherhood, a full-time job, and a chronic illness.

Respect the story behind the physique. Celebrate the struggle, not just the symmetry.

Because in this sport, the medals will fade, but the character built through discipline, sacrifice, and relentless passion? That lasts forever.

So the next time you see someone on stage, don't just admire the body. Remember the soul that built it.

Indian Bodybuilding Deserves Better

I've seen it up close — the hunger in the eyes of Indian athletes, the long hours in small gyms with no AC, the makeshift equipment, the posing practice done under flickering tube lights, and the prep meals cooked on a tight budget.

The potential? It's *everywhere.*

But the support? The structure? The recognition? *That's where we fall short.*

We're a country full of passionate, hardworking athletes. But the sad truth is — passion alone doesn't pay for coaching, supplements, travel, or show fees. Talent is not the problem. The system is. From lack of federation unity to politics in judging, from poor sponsorship to zero offseason backing — we've created a cycle where only the mentally strongest survive. And even they, often, get tired.

I've met champions who've trained with tight financials, who've won medals and returned home to zero media attention, no prize money, and not even a local gym offering them a free membership. Why?
Because we still treat bodybuilding like a niche interest — not a serious sport.

And the most heartbreaking part?

Some of the athletes we lose to the system could've been international stars if only they had the right backing. We're not lacking talent. We're lacking *management.*

In India, this fundamental knowledge is often bypassed, and that's why so many athletes struggle to reach their full potential. They have the drive, they have the passion, but without the right foundation, that drive often gets wasted.

Take, for instance, the importance of **programming**. Too many athletes—especially in India—train with the same intensity every day, thinking that more is better. But without a structured approach, their bodies never get a chance to adapt. They're stuck in a constant state of breakdown without giving their muscles the recovery time they need to grow.

I remember this one athlete who came to me—full of energy, full of ambition. He had that spark in his eyes, the kind that tells you he's serious about stepping on the big stage. Physically, he was strong. Big frame, thick muscle bellies, and the kind of strength numbers that could easily impress anyone. Deadlifts over 200 kilos, squats deep and heavy—he was proud of it all. And rightfully so. The raw strength was there. The work ethic? No doubt. But the moment he hit a few poses in front of me, something felt off.

His physique lacked symmetry. The structure just didn't flow. There was imbalance in his upper-to-lower proportions, and some muscle groups clearly overpowered others. It was one of those cases where you look at a guy and say, *"Man, he's got everything, but it's not coming together right."*

So I asked him a few simple questions—not to test him, but to understand his approach.
"Which phase of training are you in right now?"
He paused. Looked a bit unsure.
"what is your current training approach?"
He shrugged and said, *"I'm just lifting heavy and eating clean."*

Then I asked him about his offseason structure.

"What's the plan during your growth season? Do you have a timeline for your next prep? Which areas are you focusing on improving right now?"

Nothing.
He was blank. No clear offseason blueprint, no focused improvements, no programming—just day-to-day training based on how he felt.

That's when it really hit me: this guy had all the potential, but no direction.
He was like a rocket with full fuel but no navigation system.

And unfortunately, I see this a lot—especially with younger athletes. They train hard, follow intense routines, lift heavy, and eat "clean," but they have no deeper understanding of why they're doing what they're doing. No clue about programming, no assessment of weak points, no thought about phase-specific training or long-term structure. They focus on how much they can lift, not how their physique is evolving.

I sat him down and said, "Listen, you're strong, no doubt. But bodybuilding isn't just about strength. It's about balance, proportion, *flow.* That's what wins on stage."

We talked through his muscle imbalances—how his legs were overpowering his upper body, how his lats were underdeveloped compared to his chest, how his midsection needed more control during poses. He had never even analyzed himself that way. And it wasn't because he didn't care. It was simply because no one had ever taught him how to think like a pro athlete, not just train like one.

And I think that's something a lot of athletes need to hear: **You can't just train hard—you have to train with purpose.**

The *practical* side of bodybuilding—posing, peak-week strategies, and competition prep—is vital. But it should never come before **understanding** the basics of training and nutrition. Until the athlete has a strong grasp of the *science* behind what they're doing, their efforts are like trying to build a house on sand. The knowledge of **how muscles grow** and **how recovery works** is the bedrock. Without this, everything else—no matter how much time or money you put into it—is built on shaky ground.

And that's where India falls short. We have incredible athletes, but there's often a huge gap between what they *do* and what they *know.* We're in a world now where information is everywhere, but athletes often don't know where to look or how to separate the noise from the science.

The Coaches' Role: Bridging the Gap

In the West, most coaches are not just trainers—they're silent educators. They pass on knowledge as much as they pass on workout plans. They take the time to educate their athletes on biomechanics, muscle activation, recovery techniques, and even the psychology of pushing past plateaus. That's the kind of holistic coaching that makes a world of difference.

But around us, majority still focus primarily on training alone, without laying the foundation of knowledge. This lack of education doesn't just hurt the athletes—it hurts the sport as a whole. When coaches fail to provide this crucial foundation, athletes end up injured, fatigued, or burnt out long before they reach their peak potential.

You can travel across this country—from the north to the coastal towns in the south, through the crowded metros of the west and the quiet towns of the east—and there's one thing you'll hear over and over again from coaches:
"*Mujhse behtar koi nahi sikhata.*"
"I'm the best. I know it all."

It's become almost a badge of honor. This loud confidence. This belief that knowing a few scientific terms or throwing around some complicated jargon suddenly makes someone a guru of the game. You'll hear coaches confidently say things like *"I know everything about prep," or "No one conditions athletes like I do,"*

But here's the uncomfortable truth: most of them don't even know what they don't know.

It's what we call the **Dunning-Kruger effect**—a psychological phenomenon where people with low ability at something overestimate their competence. Basically, the less someone knows, the more they think they know everything. It's not arrogance alone—it's a blind spot. They've learned just enough to feel confident but not enough to realize how deep the subject truly goes.

Now here's where it gets tricky.

Some of these coaches—deep down—they **know** they don't know enough. They feel it when an athlete doesn't progress. When their plan doesn't work. When someone else steps on stage looking ten times sharper. But they can't admit it. Why?

Because they've built their entire identity around being "the coach." They've got a family to feed, a name to protect, a business to grow. So they keep repeating the same formulas, handing out the same plans, shooting the same content. They've trapped themselves in the image they created. And now, instead of learning more, they just get better at **pretending** they already know it all.

And the worst part?

Many athletes fall for it. Because when someone says something with confidence—even if it's wrong—it **sounds** like they know what they're talking about. Add some filters, a good Instagram feed, a few stage photos—and suddenly, you're "India's top prep coach."

But you know who suffers?
The athlete.

Because under all that noise, there's a lack of depth. No understanding of metabolism, no real grasp of periodization, no clue how to handle hormonal crashes, peak week water manipulations, digestion issues, or even basic posing strategy.

Let's talk about something uncomfortable — but real.

Today, a coach with a strong social media game can be seen handling 100 athletes at the same time. It sounds impressive, right? Big numbers, lots of names, multiple stage entries. And among those 100 athletes, of course, a few will win. Some will be genetic freaks. Some will have perfect response to food and training. They'll step on stage and take the gold.

And just like that — the marketing wheel starts turning. Instagram stories. Reels. Before-after shots. Taglines like *"transformed in just 8 weeks,"*

And what happens next?

Dozens of new athletes line up. DMs flood in. More sign-ups, more money, more exposure.

But here's the big question:
Do you ever stop to check the success rate?
Out of 100 athletes, how many actually win?
How many maintain their health post-show?
How many ended up injured, hormonally wrecked, mentally exhausted?

Those numbers?
They don't make it to Instagram.

You'll never see the guy who couldn't sleep for weeks post-show.
Or the girl who lost her cycle.
Or the athlete who started binge-eating because their post-show plan didn't exist.
They don't post stories. They disappear. Quietly. Silently.

This industry only shows shiny medals, but hides the cost at which they come.

And this is where things become dangerous.
Because for most athletes, **a coach becomes "No. 1" simply because they believe so.**
It's emotional.
"He got me in shape."
"I won under him."
"He's handling 100+ athletes right now."
But numbers don't mean quality.
And winning doesn't always mean well-being.

Let's put it this way —
Is the fastest car in the world always the best car?
No.
There are other things to consider — engine health, fuel efficiency, durability, safety.
Just like that, a coach isn't "the best" just because he had 10 athletes winning a show.

There's no national coaching competition.
There are no official stats.
There is no panel that ranks prep coaches by athlete health, recovery rate, long-term success, injury-free plans, optimized peak weeks, or mental well-being.

So how can we even say someone is **No. 1**?

Believing in your coach is great — in fact, it's necessary. Trust matters. But belief should be backed by **rational thought**.
Ask yourself:

- Does my coach understand me as an individual?
- Do I get feedback and communication beyond plans and PDFs?
- Do I have a long-term plan, or am I just going week-to-week?
- Is my health improving, or declining?

Because you know what? A great coach doesn't just get you stage-ready. A great coach leaves you **stronger, healthier, smarter** — after the show is over.

You have the right to trust. But also the responsibility to think.

If you're a coach reading this—this isn't to attack.
This is a call to level up.
Bodybuilding isn't a game of ego. It's a science. An art. A process. And just because you've coached a few winners or read a few articles doesn't mean you've reached the top. In fact, if you really want to serve your athletes—**you have to unlearn first, and then relearn again and again.**

The best coaches I've seen? They're quiet observers. Always listening. Always studying. They admit when they don't know something. They ask other experts. They keep their head down and focus on **progress**, not popularity.

To my Athlete Community

If someone is always trying to prove they're the best—they probably aren't. The best don't scream. They teach, they guide, and they **stay students for life**.

Don't be impressed by loud words.
Instead of looking only at the Medal on stage, look at the **athlete's health**, their **improvements over time**, the way they **pose**, the way their **mind-set is shaped**. A true coach builds not just the body but the **person behind the body**.

So, what's the solution? How do we bridge this gap and truly elevate Indian bodybuilding?

First, it's about giving **athletes the tools** to build knowledge. Coaches need to go beyond just programming exercises. They need to be **educators**. They need to teach their athletes how and why their bodies respond to training, how nutrition fuels performance, and how recovery makes the difference between success and burnout.

Second, **athletes** themselves need to take ownership of their education. It's not enough to show up, train, and expect results. You have to understand *why* things are working and *why* they're not. Read, research, ask questions. Knowledge, when applied correctly, is just as powerful as strength. Maybe even more so.

And finally, as a community, we need to shift our focus from just the "show" to the *process*. In India, we love to celebrate the final result—the medal, the title, the fame. But we often forget that those results aren't just luck. They're built from hours of learning, adapting, and mastering the art of training. **The journey of knowledge, when combined with relentless practice, is what turns potential into greatness.**

Almost every athlete you see on stage today — the shredded ones, the strong ones, even the ones holding trophies — they didn't start their journey in big gyms or with celebrity coaches. Most of them came from small, basic gyms. I believe that the **foundation of our bodybuilding culture is broken** in many places. Not because athletes don't have passion. But because the **right education, guidance, and support is missing from the very beginning**.

1. A Good Start Can Change Everything

I've seen boys with amazing genetics — broad shoulders, tight waists, fast muscle response. They could've been something huge. But they started with the wrong kind of coaching. Nobody taught them about food, training, recovery, or health.

So they wasted their early years. And once that time is gone, you don't get it back.

But imagine — if these athletes met someone who actually understood science, health, and long-term planning right from the beginning... They wouldn't just win shows — they'd rule the sport. That's how important a good start is.

2. The Shortcut Culture

Everyone Wants Results, But Nobody Wants to Invest. Bodybuilding is not a cheap sport. It needs good food, proper recovery, supplements, posing practice, and guidance. But many athletes don't want to spend on quality things. They'll ask for free coaching, skip meals, take shortcuts, or look for cheaper alternatives. And the saddest part? **They're risking their health** — just to save a few hundred rupees.

3. Money Matters, Spend Wisely

Many claim the sport is financially crushing, but the reality is, it's often the choices, not the requirements, that inflate the costs. The difference between a manageable budget and an overwhelming one often comes down to decision-making. Too many athletes fall into the trap of believing that the most expensive supplement, coach, or gear automatically translates to better results. It doesn't. What truly matters is understanding your individual needs and aligning them with sound, practical guidance. The right mentor won't push you toward excess—they'll help you strip away the noise and focus on what actually delivers results: consistent training, calculated nutrition, smart recovery, and patience. Managing good food, supplements, blood work, show expenses — it takes a lot. Some athletes work two jobs, borrow money, and skip essentials— just to stay in the game. And it breaks my heart. This is why they sometimes settle for less.

4. Social Media is Misleading

Coaches post their top 1-2 winners and promote them everywhere. But what about the rest who didn't do well?

What about those who struggled with health issues, post-show depression, digestion problems, or hormone crashes?

They don't show that. Because it doesn't look good in reels.

And that's the trap — athletes only see the medals. Not the pain behind it.

They think, "He made a champion, he'll make me one too." But not every plan works for everybody. And not every journey is healthy just because it ends in a medal.

5. Changing Coaches Like T-Shirts

I've seen athletes change 2-3 coaches in one season. No one sits down to understand if the coach actually suits their body type, mindset, or goal.

They pick whoever is close, confident, and cheap or someone who promise them big rewards. Sometimes even someone who promises magic in 8 weeks.

That's not how bodybuilding works. It takes time. It takes trust. It takes real communication.

A good coach-athlete relationship is like a partnership — built over time. But now, many are just chasing fast fame with anyone who sounds "convincing."

6. Where is the Support System?

This is what hurts me the most — **athletes don't have anywhere to go for guidance.**

There are no proper discussion meets, open counselling platforms, or safe spaces where they can talk freely, ask doubts, or share struggles.

They suffer in silence.
They don't tell anyone if they're feeling low.
They don't speak up when something feels wrong.
And in this silence, so many good athletes lose direction.

If Indian bodybuilding truly wants to rise, we need to fix things **from the ground up**.

It need a system where:

- Every small gym has basic education on nutrition and training.
- Every athlete learns about his genetics and health before taking substances.
- Coaches are selected based on knowledge, not just confidence and marketing.
- Money doesn't decide the quality of guidance.
- And most importantly, athletes have **support, education, and safety**.

Because it's not just about trophies.

It's about building a generation that is **strong, smart, and healthy** — not just on stage, but in life.

The Future of Judging, Education, and Athlete Advocacy

I still remember the call. It was just after a small local show, nothing big, but important to us. It was my athlete playing for the first time—

young, new to competing, I picked up, and before I could say anything, he blurted out—

"Sir... they didn't even let us pose!"

His voice was all over the place—upset, confused, kind of shaky. Like he was trying not to cry but also trying to act tough. I asked him what happened.

"Sir, they were so fast. Like, we got on stage, and only 4 poses and done. We were not asked to complete all poses. It was like they were in a hurry or something!"

I could hear the frustration bubbling up. He wasn't angry at the placing—he hadn't even looked at it yet. He just felt ignored.

"I worked so hard for this, Coach. I was holding my poses, trying to do everything right like we practiced, and it was like they didn't care. We were standing in the back like we were invisible."

Then there was this long pause. And then he said something that hit me hard.

"I don't even know why I went up there. What was the point if no one's even looking?"

How many times have I told people, *"Just bring your best, and the judges will see it"?*

But is that even true anymore?

That night, I made myself a promise. Not something loud or dramatic—just quiet. Just in my own head. A line I drew for myself.

If I ever had a voice big enough in this sport... I'd use it.
Not to complain. Not to argue with people or talk politics.
But to make sure we *see* them.
All of them. Every athlete.

I'm talking about the kid who saved up every rupee for his first prep. The single mom stepping on stage after so much struggle. The guy who lost 30 kilos and finally feels like he belongs.

Because bodybuilding isn't just about shredded glutes or perfect symmetry. It's about the story behind that body. The sacrifice. The hunger. The struggle. The discipline no one sees behind the stage lights.

And if we stop noticing that—if we stop seeing the people behind the physiques—then what are we even doing? We lose the whole point.

So yeah, I still carry that moment with me. Every single show. When I'm judging, when I'm backstage, when I see a nervous first-timer adjusting their trunk—I remember.

For them, this isn't just a show.
It's everything.

It's time we start asking a hard question: *Who's really judging the judges?* Because as this sport grows, so does the responsibility of those who decide its outcomes. And if we want bodybuilding to evolve, we need a new generation of judges—people who are not just passionate about the sport, but truly *qualified* to uphold its values. Judges with real educational backgrounds, who understand anatomy, physiology, biomechanics—not just posing angles. People with technical expertise who can back their decisions with logic, not bias. We need professionals who have strong communication skills, who can handle critical conversations with athletes and coaches, and who aren't afraid to give honest, constructive feedback. Time management, emotional control, and pressure handling are essential too—because shows are chaotic, and judges must remain composed, fair, and focused. Most importantly, we need people with the courage to stay true to ethics. Brave enough to resist favoritism, politics, or behind-the-scenes influence.

We are all, at the end of the day, human. And humans are biased creatures.
Philosopher and psychologist **Daniel Kahneman**—Nobel Prize winner and author of *Thinking, Fast and Slow*—has shown that even highly trained professionals fall prey to unconscious bias. Our brains love shortcuts. They want to make fast decisions. And in a lineup of 15 physiques, those shortcuts show up *fast.*

You might favor someone in the center of the stage (the "center bias"), even before you really assess them. You might place someone higher because you recognize them from Instagram or past shows (the "fame effect" or "recency bias"). You might reward someone for being leaner, even if they lack proportion—because your eye is trained to admire sharp conditioning over balance. This is called the **salience bias**—we notice what's loud, even if it's not right.

But *that* is exactly why competence must go hand in hand with self-awareness. A good judge trains their *mind* as much as their eye. They know how to pause before reacting. They learn to recognize their own cognitive biases—like the halo effect (where one good trait overshadows flaws), or confirmation bias (seeing only what we want to see). True judging requires emotional discipline, and the humility to question your own instincts. A judge doesn't just hold a clipboard—they hold responsibility. And that responsibility should never be taken lightly.

So what makes a good judge?

Not just someone who knows the rulebook—but someone who has trained their *mind* as much as their eye.

We need judges who have:

- **Critical thinking skills** – Who can stop, reassess, and question their own initial reactions.
- **Self-awareness** – Who understand how bias works and actively try to correct for it.
- **Emotional regulation** – Who can stay calm under pressure, during long pre-judging rounds, last-minute comparisons, or even athlete protests.
- **Time and stress management** – Because judging isn't done in a calm room with music and coffee. It's done in loud venues, tight schedules, and emotional atmospheres.
- **Communication skills** – Not just for giving feedback, but for *owning their decision-making.* A judge should be able to say, "Here's

why I placed you where I did," with clarity and without defensiveness.

- **Ethical courage** – To resist favoritism, politics, and behind-the-scenes influence. To stand alone, if needed, for the right call.

Training the Judge, Not Just the Athlete

If we can create structured judging certifications—real programs with ongoing evaluation, education in human bias, posing, lighting, psychology, and athlete management—we can build a culture of trust.

Athletes should feel judged by professionals, not personalities.

And federations? They should take responsibility for developing and mentoring judges who align with their criteria, who communicate well, and who hold themselves to the same level of accountability we expect from the athletes they score.

I remember one evening, sitting down with an older, very experienced judge—someone who's seen it all, been through every generation of bodybuilders, and judged countless shows. We were discussing the rise of divisions like Classic Physique and Men's Physique, and he turned to me and said something that struck me deep. He said, "You know, I've been in this game a long time, but I'll be honest—we still don't fully understand what Classic Physique or Men's Physique are supposed to look like."

We have a whole generation of judges who were great back in their time. They coached, competed, and judged under a completely different set of standards. *Classic Physique* and *Men's Physique* weren't even concepts when they were at their peak. So, understandably, their reference points are stuck in the past. When they look at the current divisions, they see something they never had to account for before. And if they don't invest time in truly understanding these evolving categories—studying the criteria, talking to experts, attending seminars, and opening their minds to the changes—they're left behind.

Here's the core of the issue: The criteria for these divisions are *constantly evolving*. Each year, we see changes in what's considered ideal. A more refined eye is needed, one that understands the flow and structure of Classic Physique or the marketability and charisma that judges look for in Men's Physique. What was once considered the "ideal" physique has shifted, and if a judge refuses to acknowledge that shift, they risk making decisions based on outdated standards.

There's an old saying: *"If you want to learn, learn from the best, because there's less room for error."*

But in bodybuilding, we're seeing a dangerous trend where experience is being equated with infallibility. That's where the problem starts. Just because someone has been judging for years doesn't mean they've been doing it right for years. Experience is only valuable when it's paired with the *right* actions and the *right mindset*. The truth is, experience is about doing the right things repeatedly, not just doing things over and over. As Aristotle once said, *"We are what we repeatedly do. Excellence, then, is not an act, but a habit."*

In the industry, what's often frustrating is that it's not always about striving for excellence—it's about sticking to old habits. You'll find judges, some with decades of experience, still making decisions based on the physiques that worked in their time—back when Classic Physique didn't even exist, and Men's Physique wasn't even a thought. They're judging based on what they know, even though the sport has moved on and evolved.

What's even worse is the reluctance to ask questions or admit that maybe they don't fully understand the newer divisions. Instead of reaching out to those who are more in tune with the current trends and requirements, many judges choose to stay in their comfort zone. They keep judging in the same old way, even if it doesn't match where the sport is heading.

The real danger here is that when you're stuck in your own bubble, only hearing opinions that match your own, you stop growing. You're not learning from others or challenging your own perspective. Instead, you're just reinforcing your limited view, making it harder to stay relevant in the ever-changing world of bodybuilding.

There's a clear lesson here. In order to judge fairly and accurately, we must evolve. We must invest time in learning and adapting. A judge's responsibility goes beyond experience—it requires an active commitment to staying updated, to understanding the philosophy behind the changes in the sport, and to continually challenging one's own biases. The mindset has to shift from, *"I've seen it all"* to, *"I'm always learning."*

This isn't just about judging physiques—it's about respecting the athletes who put in the work to meet *today's* standards. And we, as judges, need to make sure we're holding ourselves to the same standard.

Jean-Paul Sartre, a prominent existentialist philosopher, once said, "**Existence precedes essence**." What this means is that it's the story, the effort, the journey—the actions and struggles—that truly define a person. And I believe this applies to bodybuilding as well. When we judge an athlete, we need to remember that they are more than just their appearance. They're the product of countless hours of hard work, sacrifice, and a level of commitment that often goes unspoken. That's what truly makes them who they are, not just how they look in a physique contest.

One of the most important roles in athlete advocacy is for judges to provide clarity in their decisions. Too often, judging is reduced to a simple "rank them from 1 to 10" approach, without offering the feedback that could guide an athlete's next steps. This leaves athletes in the dark, confused about what they need to improve, or even worse, feeling overlooked altogether.

Imagine, for a moment, a young athlete—perhaps this is their first show, or their first show in a while. They've worked tirelessly for months, sometimes years, getting their body in shape, perfecting their posing, dialing in their nutrition. They wait for the results, hoping to hear their name called. But when it isn't, they don't know why.

They didn't hear anything about their conditioning, their posing, and their symmetry. All they got was a sheet with their name and a number. That's it. No feedback. No insight.

This is where the power of advocacy comes in. Judges must be able to communicate their decisions with the athletes, offering constructive criticism and guidance. This isn't just a favor—it's an essential part of the process. It helps athletes grow, and it builds trust in the system.

While judges play a pivotal role in athlete advocacy, coaches are often the first line of defense. A coach is not just someone who trains an athlete to perform—they are a guide, a mentor, and sometimes, a sounding board for the emotional and mental challenges that come with being a competitor.

Experience at the Last show I visited

I remember this one show I went to with one of my amateur athletes. We were just there, talking to some friends and catching up with people we knew. Then, out of nowhere, the organizer called me over. "Hey, can you come take a look at the comparison for Classic Physique?" he asked. I nodded and made my way over to the Judges Table.

Now, when you've been in the game for as long as I have, you've seen it all. And as I stood behind the Judges, I couldn't help but overhear the conversations around me. "Look at his conditioning, look at his hamstrings," someone said. Another voice chimed in, "His abs are dense." And I couldn't help but shake my head, amused by the conversation unfolding around me. It's always the same thing—people focusing on one or two visible features, thinking that's the whole picture. But it's never that simple.

Conditioning, hamstrings, abs—sure, they matter. But what about everything else? The balance, the symmetry, the posing flow, muscle maturity, and the overall presentation? All those things matter just as much, if not more. What frustrated me more than anything was the bias. People get locked into their preferences, wanting to see certain things and ignoring the bigger picture. It's not about what's superior to you as an individual; it's about how all those variables work together. A true judge, or anyone with an eye for detail, understands that.

And this is something I've learned over the years: when you start a conversation with someone, within seconds you can tell whether they're open-minded or just stuck in their own narrow perspective. That's what I realized as I stood there. Most people were so caught up in their own biases that there was no room for deeper discussion.

When you're dead, it doesn't hurt you — it hurts everyone else. Stupidity works the same way. There's no point in engaging with that kind of mind set. You have to let it go.

After a while, I turned to the organizer, gave him my thoughts, and then walked away. I already knew who was going to win. We live in a world where we can read the room, understand the dynamics, connections, and know what's really going on beneath the surface. When you understand that, you can see the winner even before the final judgment is made.

Message to the Reader

If you've made it this far, I want to take a moment to thank you. Writing this wasn't easy. Not because the truth is hard to tell, but because I never wanted to be misunderstood.

Whether you're an athlete, a coach, or someone who just feels connected to the world of bodybuilding, I hope something in this book resonated with you. I wrote this to bring more understanding, not noise. If this added even a little perspective or clarity to your journey, then I'm grateful.

Bodybuilding isn't just about trophies, medals, or even the stage. It's about who you become in the process. It's about building not just muscle, but mental strength that can carry you through life's hardest moments.

I hope the bodybuilding community continues to grow stronger, kinder, and more united and I truly wish success to everyone out there putting in the work.

Let's keep growing—because the journey never ends.

With gratitude,

Sunil Sheoran